# MURDER IN THE CAYMAN ISLANDS

## A Northwest Cozy Mystery - Book 9

BY

DIANNE HARMAN

Published by: Dianne Harman
www.dianneharman.com

Interior, cover design and website by
Vivek Rajan

Paperback ISBN: 9781731405234

# CONTENTS

Acknowledgments

1   Prologue       1

2   Chapter One       8

3   Chapter Two       15

4   Chapter Three       22

5   Chapter Four       29

6   Chapter Five       37

7   Chapter Six       45

8   Chapter Seven       51

9   Chapter Eight       58

10   Chapter Nine       65

11   Chapter Ten       72

12   Chapter Eleven       79

13   Chapter Twelve       86

14   Chapter Thirteen       92

15   Chapter Fourteen       99

16   Chapter Fifteen       106

17   Chapter Sixteen       114

18   Chapter Seventeen       122

19   Chapter Eighteen       129

| 20 | Epilogue | 138 |
| 21 | Recipes | 143 |
| 22 | About Dianne | 148 |
| 23 | Coming Soon | 149 |

## ACKNOWLEDGMENTS

To all of the people who help get my books published, thank you!

And to all of the people who read my books, thank you!

## Win FREE Paperbacks every week!

Go to www.dianneharman.com/freepaperback.html and get your FREE copies of Dianne's books and favorite recipes immediately by signing up for her newsletter.

Once you've signed up for her newsletter you're eligible to win three paperbacks. One lucky winner is picked every week. Hurry before the offer ends!

# PROLOGUE

Nicky Luchesse inhaled the fresh salt air and felt a whisper of afternoon breeze against his leathery tanned skin. He threw a length of a mooring line from his boat onto the wooden dock and then jumped off the Sunseeker Manhattan 52, his long legs clearing the water between the boat and the dock with ease.

The Sunseeker, a luxurious runabout for cruising the local waters, was just one of the many boats Nicky owned. Other days, when he had more time on his hands, he loved to take one of his sailboats out to sea with no destination in mind.

*Yes, sailing boats are the pleasure of my life,* Nicky thought to himself, *but I'll never forget, it can all be snatched away in an instant.* Today's trip, however, had not been about pleasure. It had been strictly about business.

Landing on the dock with a thud, his well-worn Top-Sider boat shoes worn over his bare feet ensured he didn't slip. He tied the boat up to the dock with a bowline knot, ensuring that the lines were secure. Nicky had no children—his boats were his babies. He cared for his vessels with as much love as one would for a newborn child.

Hurricane season was coming to an end in the Cayman Island, but he wasn't taking any chances with loose moorings. He tied them short and tight. He paid a crew to always be on hand if needed, but he liked doing it himself. That way, if something went wrong, he only had himself to blame. He was aware he'd taken his eye off the ball in his business recently, and now he was having to deal with the mess that had been created. He wasn't taking the same chance with one of his precious boats.

A voice called to him from the deck of the boat. Bob, one of his most trusted crew members, was in the process of stacking wooden crates of cargo on the deck of the boat. It was the kind that didn't get declared at border control. "Jevaun should be here soon. I'll wait to supervise the handover." He nodded towards the boxes. "Anything else, Skipper?"

Nicky shook his head. "No, you can finish for the day when he gets here. There's twelve boxes, right?"

Bob did a quick recount, moving his finger in the air. "Yeah."

Nicky chuckled. "Good. You know there's twelve, I know there's twelve, now we need to make sure Jevaun knows that we know there's twelve, if you get me. Too many boxes have been going missing lately. When I get to the bottom of that little mystery, someone's going to find themselves paying a visit to Davy Jones' locker."

"Aye, aye." Bob said with a grin, his bright white teeth standing out in contrast to the color of his ebony skin. "Don't worry, I'll tell him."

Nicky finished fixing the boat lines and straightened up. "Good. I'm going up to the house. Bring Princess Leia in the morning, will you? I'm going fishing. A friend of mine's in town."

"Must be a good friend, if you're taking them on the Princess. She's your pride and joy." Bob said as he sat down on top of one of the stacks of cargo crates that were lined up three deep on the deck.

"That she is." Nicky took off his baseball cap and grinned. "And yes, it's a very good friend. Al De Duco, you've met him. See you tomorrow, Bob."

Princess Leia, a 75' Sunreef Sportfish, was the biggest luxury catamaran-yacht available in the fishing version in the world. It was designed for deep sea fishing enthusiasts who appreciated the catamaran benefits of stability, low draft, and long range. That, coupled with low fuel consumption and extensive storage, made it perfect for shallow or deep-water fishing in warm or cold climates. Al would love her.

Nicky walked up the private dock that extended from the end of his property out over the turquoise water, his thick silver mane of hair shining in the sunlight. His business partner, Benny, mocked him for having hair hitting his shoulders at his age, but Nicky laughed off his jibes with good humor. What anyone thought of him simply wasn't important to Nicky. And Benny, after two failed hair transplants and still as bald as a billiard ball, didn't have any room to talk.

Nicky pulled his phone out of his pocket and pressed in Benny's number.

"Bob's got the candy," he said when Benny picked up. They talked in code in case the line was bugged.

Benny's deep voice boomed down the line. "Excellent. Fancy a beer? I just landed from Miami, and I'll be heading your way in a little while. A twenty says there's two bar stools with our names on them at Calico Jack's on Seven Mile Beach. I can pick you up. We need to talk. I'm starting to think you've been avoiding me."

Nicky checked his watch. "No can do, Benny, my man. I've got company coming, and I'm about to get ready for them."

He heard Benny puff on a cigar. Benny and cigars were like pancakes and maple syrup. Benny was sweeter when he had one in his hand.

"A lady friend, by any chance? Which one's it to be tonight,

Nicky? It's a wonder their paths haven't crossed."

"Don't I know it, Benny." Nicky's relationship status could be summed up in two words. "It's complicated." There had been more than one close call when the two women in Nicky's life had almost bumped into each other, but so far, he'd managed to get away with it. That was something else he needed to sort out. He hadn't been paying proper attention to his love life, and it had gotten out of hand as well.

"Maybe you should quit playing games. If you don't, one of these days they're going to find out what you've been up to and you'll risk losing them both."

"You're right, Benny." Nicky strode across the rolling lawn towards the large white stucco house hidden from the road by a wrought-iron fence and a colorful hibiscus hedge. The garden was filled with tropical flowers, and the scent of both bougainvillea and Barbados poinciana filled the air. Trees bowed with the weight of ripening mangos and bananas, and he had to step over several pieces of fruit which had fallen on the grass. "It's been on my mind for a while. I'm well aware that one of them has to go."

Benny's voice turned cold. "Listen, Nicky, forget the small talk. It's about the boat, and wh…"

Nicky cut him off with an exasperated sigh. "This is getting old, Benny. Can we talk about it tomorrow? The guest I've got coming ain't of the goodlookin' variety, although he'd probably dispute that. He's an old friend of yours from Chicago, come to think of it. A couple of years older than us, used to be in the Gambino family before he retired. Remember Vinny and Al?"

Benny mumbled in Italian, *God rest Vinny's soul*, before switching back to English. "Course I do. Legends in our lifetime. Al de Duco, huh? I forgot he's got a place down here. Last I heard, he was playing happy families over Seattle way. Happens to the best of them, I guess. When's he due at your place? I remember the time we…"

Nicky rolled his eyes as Benny recounted an incident with Al accidentally firing his gun in a hardware store. There was no such thing as a quick conversation with Benny. He could talk all day about the grass growing, the traffic or lack of it, or which way the wind was blowing just to hear the sound of his own voice.

"Al's due in about an hour, Benny, with his new wife and some friends from Seattle. I'm taking them for a quick spin on the cruiser before hosting dinner here. Tell you what, why don't you come over first thing in the morning? I'm planning on taking the Princess out for the day, but you and me can talk before I go. Come fishing with us, if you like. Al would love to see you."

Nicky wasn't able to decipher whether the grunt from Benny's end of the line was affirmative or not. He tried another tack. "Benny, I know you're mad about what happened with the last candy delivery, but maybe it'll show up. In fact, the candy man is on his way to meet Bob right now. Why don't I speak to him again, see if he can't find it after all? I can let you know what he says in the morning."

"Mad don't even come close, Nicky. Tell the candy man for me that there's no more time. Same goes for you. Benny just ran out of patience." The line went dead.

Nicky stared at his phone. He was used to his business partner's moods blowing hot and cold and was inclined to shrug it off. They'd both been stung by the loss of the last shipment, worth a seven-figure amount. It didn't help that Jevaun was looking for Benny and him to cover the cost of his fishing boat that had been carrying the cargo. The small matter of the insurance having lapsed didn't sit well with them either. Once Nicky had checked on dinner, he'd have to go back to the dock to try and get some straight answers from Jevaun.

He entered the house by the back door, and stepped into the kitchen to make sure his housekeeper, Sharisha, had fixed everything for dinner. Smiling at the spread of olive and cheese appetizers, seafood chowder, bolla bread, and for dessert, cassava cake, he read the accompanying note on the counter with heating instructions.

"Thank you, Sharisha," he said to the empty kitchen.

Nicky had given the staff the afternoon off before he'd gone out with Bob, knowing they wouldn't let him down. He climbed the stairs and went into his bedroom. There, on the bed, were freshly pressed chinos and a polo shirt which Sharisha had laid out for him.

In the shower, he stood under the jets aiming at him from above and allowed them to soak his hair. He rolled his shoulders and soaped his body as the jets on the walls shot steaming water against his back and his chest, easing his aching joints. Although he was physically fit for a man in his sixties, he could always feel his age at the end of a day on the water. This time of year, when the weather turned cooler, arthritis racked his body.

There was no question of him slowing down, but Nicky sometimes wondered if his life couldn't be simpler. The decades of Chicago winters having taken their toll, he'd moved to the Cayman Island for the weather. His work was still on the wrong side of the law, but as long as he was careful, no one bothered him here. Benny took care of the shipments when they arrived in Miami. Lately, with the Jevaun situation, Nicky wondered if they didn't need a backup plan. If Jevaun couldn't be trusted, they'd need to make other arrangements. The problem was, getting rid of Jevaun could be tricky. Maybe an accident at sea would be appropriate.

*Benny knows all about those,* Nicky thought with a smile.

Socially, Nicky was much in demand. His own vanity had gotten him into the situation in which he now found himself, with two beautiful women vying for his affections. Not that either of them knew they had competition, or so he hoped. The problem was, if he had to choose, he wasn't sure who it would be. Lady Gwen, the English aristocrat, or Devan, the local beauty with eyes as bright as diamonds and a smile that would melt a snowman. He knew a lot of men would be very happy to be in his dilemma. As he stepped out of the shower and dried himself off, he decided to leave that conundrum for another day.

When Nicky approached the dock half an hour later, a beer in his hand and his still-wet hair resting on his shoulders, he thought *Life doesn't get much better than this.*

In the distance, the cruiser bobbed on the water, beyond that an expanse of crystal blue stretched as far as the eye could see. A flight of birds passed overhead, and Nicky squinted in the fading sunlight trying to determine the breed of the large one in front. A gun shot rang out through the air, piercing the serene silence.

*Never forget, it can all be snatched away in an instant.*

And then it turned dark for Nicky.

# CHAPTER ONE

"Al wasn't wrong when he said the view from this hotel is amazing," DeeDee Rogers said as she stood on the balcony of their twelfth-floor hotel room at the Hilton Miami Airport Blue Lagoon "It's like being on our own little island, and admittedly, a very fancy one."

Her husband, Jake, stepped beside her, snaking an arm around her waist. "And we know how much you like islands."

DeeDee turned to him and grinned. "That I do. I'm an island girl, through and through." Their home was on Bainbridge Island in Washington, although they were living temporarily on the east coast. As if reading her mind, Jake pulled her closer and kissed her tenderly. "I know how much you miss Bainbridge, sweetheart, and especially being away from your sister and her new twins. But we both know we won't be in Connecticut for much longer."

They looked at each other in silence as each of them contemplated the meaning behind his words. DeeDee turned away to again admire their view. Jake was temporarily working in Connecticut to cover a friend's private investigation business because his wife was terminally ill. As much as DeeDee wanted to return to Bainbridge Island, if they did, it would mean bad news for the family they'd come to help.

"I've come to think of Trent and Michelle as friends," she said carefully. "When we leave, after she passes away, and I know it won't be long now till…my feelings will be tinged with sadness."

She thought of Trent and Michelle's three children and the fear she'd seen in their eyes as they watched their mother's health deteriorate. The two older children, teenage boys, were better at hiding it. But at six, Mila, the baby of the family, was full of questions, and not so good at dealing with the answers, no matter how gently they were framed.

"Mila loves Balto," DeeDee sniffed. "It will break her heart all over again when we take him back home with us and away from her."

Jake rubbed her back. "She can come visit," he said softly. "And she's so happy to be in charge of a dog and looking after him while we take this short vacation."

DeeDee nodded, bowing her head to wipe away a tear that had trickled down her cheek. The invitation to spend a week on Grand Cayman with their friends, Al and Cassie De Duco, couldn't have come at a better time. She knew that Jake, although he hadn't said anything, was feeling the pressure too.

This break was just what they needed to decompress, recharge their batteries, and spend some quality time together. What with Jake working around the clock and DeeDee helping Trent with the cooking and the children, while he cared for Michelle, there hadn't been a lot of time to concentrate on their own marriage, which was still new.

The telephone on the nightstand rang, and she looked up at Jake with a half-smile. "That'll be Al. You'd better get it. You know he doesn't like to be kept waiting for dinner. I'll go freshen up."

Jake kissed her on the forehead and walked over to the nightstand to pick up the house phone. She heard him say, "Hey, Al, what's up?" before turning to her with a wink as she made her way to the bathroom.

*****

When they got off the elevator and walked into the lobby half an hour later, DeeDee could hear Al before she saw him. She exchanged a glance with Jake, who supressed a smile. They followed the sound of Al's voice to a sofa by the window, which looked out onto a garden where small lights in the trees and bushes twinkled in the evening darkness.

"Ima tellin' ya', Cassie," Al was saying as he pointed to the drinks on the table, "this cocktail is for cissies. Ima not drinkin' anything with some fancy umbrella in it. Ima gonna' order somethin' else."

When they got closer, Cassie saw them first, and jumped up to greet them with outstretched arms. "DeeDee!" She flung her arms around DeeDee while Al stood up to shake hands with Jake, who then kissed Cassie while DeeDee found herself wrapped up in one of Al's well-known bear hugs.

"Nice to see you too, Al," she laughed when she'd extracted herself from his embrace. She patted herself down. "Let me just check and make sure that no bones are broken."

"Here," Al said, handing her a cocktail glass containing a frothy concoction with a cherry on a stick and an umbrella in it. A wedge of pineapple was stuck on the rim of the glass. "We already ordered you a drink. Me and Jake are gonna' have a whisky, right, Jake?"

Jake nodded, and DeeDee accepted the glass with a polite murmur, catching Cassie rolling her eyes at Al. She took a sip through the straw and smiled. "Yum, Pina Colada, my favorite. Good memory, Al."

Al had the decency to look somewhat bashful. "It's the house Happy Hour special. Watch out ya' don't get plastered," he said with a grunt, before turning to Cassie. "That goes for you, too. I don't want either of ya' complainin' about headaches when we get to Grand Cayman tomorrow."

"Yes, Al," DeeDee said with a giggle, while Al signaled to the waiter to order his and Jake's drinks. "We promise."

As DeeDee chatted with Cassie, the stress of the last few months faded into the background. While the men talked about work, DeeDee and Cassie had more than enough other things to catch up on. It seemed like only a few minutes had passed when Al interrupted them with a nudge of his elbow into Cassie's side.

"If you two can quit gassin' about shoppin', children, and recipes fer a few minutes, maybe we can go inta the restaurant and have dinner? All that talk about food is makin' me and Jake hungry."

DeeDee glanced at her watch in surprise. "Sorry, guys, we didn't realize we'd been, um, gassing for quite so long." She looked up at Jake, whose face was twitching listening to Al. Her heart skipped a beat as his piercing bright blue eyes met hers, causing a wave of happiness to flood over her. With the man she loved by her side, she knew with certainty they could get through anything. Spending time with great friends like Al and Cassie was frosting on the cake.

They stood up, and DeeDee linked her arm through Jake's as they made their way into the dining room. A bottle of champagne was waiting in an ice bucket on a stand at the side of the table where they were seated by the hostess.

"What's this, are we celebrating something?" Jake asked, pulling DeeDee's chair out for her before sitting beside her.

Al grinned. "We sure are." He indicated for the waiter to fill their glasses. "It ain't every day Cassie and me gets to spend time with two of our most favorite people. We wanted to thank you for agreein' to come on this trip with us. Oh, and Red does too."

DeeDee smiled. "The pleasure is all ours. Balto sends his love. He's sorry he couldn't make it, but he got a better offer, from a six-year-old, no less."

Al raised his glass and cleared his throat. "I'd like to propose a toast. To friends, absent dogs, and to catchin' some really big fish."

"And no murders," Cassie added as they clinked glasses.

"Definitely no murders," Al said with a solemn face. "You'll see jes' how laid-back the lifestyle is in the Caymans when we get there. It's a happy place. I think of our home there as a little piece of paradise." He paused and smiled at Cassie. "It's the perfect getaway destination when you need a break from the real world. That's why I was plannin' on livin' there until Cassie turned my head."

Cassie lifted a bread roll and pretended to aim it at Al.

"Thanks," he said, prying the roll from her grip and breaking it with his fingers. "I know a few people where we're goin', so there's always someone to have a cold one with. My pal, Nicky, has already invited us over tomorrow evenin' fer dinner. I think you'll like him. He's quite an interestin' guy. He knows the best fishin' spots and can probably tell you ladies which boutiques are worth a look-see. I'm sure he spends a pretty penny in them for his lady friends."

DeeDee spoke up. "Does Nicky work there, Al, or is he retired?"

Al popped a chunk of bread in his mouth and chewed. When he was done, he looked at his menu. "Oh, he works, all right. Maybe we should order? Cuz' if Jake dies of hunger, we're in trouble."

"Yep, second-degree murder kind of trouble," Jake said.

Cassie laughed. "Fine. I think I'd like the maple-brined pork chops with pear chutney and the confetti salad."

"You always pick the same as I do, Cassie," DeeDee said with a sigh.

Jake snapped his menu shut. "Easy choice. It's calamari for an appetizer and chateaubriand for me."

"My turn to copy you," Al said to Jake with a grin.

The waiter arrived at the table and topped off their champagne glasses before taking their orders.

"What line of work is Nicky in?" Jake asked, when the waiter had gone. "Finance?"

Al chuckled. "Ya' probably don't want to know about that, Jake. Let's just say he knows his way in and out of smugglers coves for a reason."

Jake groaned. "You're right, and I never heard that. I forgot that your friends are usually a colorful lot. I'm sure he's a pleasant guy, but some things don't sit well with me. Don't say any more, and we'll forget all about it."

"Good idea." Al looked at Jake with a good-natured smile. "That's one of the things I like about ya', Jake. You're not shy 'bout sayin' what ya' think. I know ya' don't approve of my past, and I'm not sure I do either, but it is what it is. I like to think everyone has a little bit of good in 'em, even if they do bad things."

Cassie slid her hand across the table and placed it on top of Al's.

From where she was sitting opposite from them, DeeDee thought she could see Al's eyes well up. "I guess we all have to meet our maker," Al went on. "And maybe I'm not gettin' through the pearly gates when I get there. Karma's a thing. Jes' ask Vinny." He swallowed and made the sign of the cross with his right hand.

Jake looked him straight in the eye. "Al, do you think we'd all be sitting here if we didn't hold you in the highest regard?"

"Don't go gettin' all soppy on me," Al mumbled. "I just want ya'll to know I've got your backs, that's all."

"You already showed us that, Al," DeeDee said. "And we'll be eternally grateful." She was referring to the time her life had been threatened after a murder on New Year's Eve earlier that year, when Al had protected her as well as helping to apprehend the killer.

"If we're havin' a heart-to-heart, maybe I should confess I mighta' had an ulterior motive that time. When I came to yer' rescue, I mean." Al adjusted the tinted sunglasses that were a permanent feature on his face wherever he went, day or night.

"When the call came from Jake askin' fer help, I was kinda' hopin' to meet that friend of yours that was sittin' at Vinny's table at your sister Roz's weddin'. And whaddya' know? She was at your place the night I arrived." He grinned at Cassie. "I couldn't have planned it better."

Cassie's mouth fell open. "You...are you serious?" She glanced down at the bread basket, but it was empty.

Al shrugged and DeeDee, watching in amusement, was unable to tell whether he was joking or not.

"Saved by the food, I think," Jake said with a smile, as the waiter approached their table with their dinner entreés.

# CHAPTER TWO

Devan Parker toyed with the chunky gold chain on her slender wrist and rotated one of the charms dangling from its links, a miniature cat with diamond encrusted eyes. The charm next to it was a mini gold cell phone with diamonds for the buttons. The remaining charms dotted around the bracelet shared the same theme, their jewels sparkling in the rays of the late afternoon sun.

Despite the envious glances she received from some of the women sitting nearby, Devan was embarrassed by what she considered the bracelet's sparse number of charms. She wouldn't be happy until her arm was weighted down by a lot more of them. Nicky had bought her the chain when they started seeing each other, adding a charm every Christmas and birthday for the last five years. Her hints about speeding up the process of completing the charm collection fell on deaf ears. Nicky liked to keep her dangling, just like those exquisite, one-of-a-kind charms.

She crossed her long, elegant legs and watched Nicky carry drinks over to their table. Nicky liked going to the bar himself. The table service could be very slow. "Makes me feel like a local," he said. Just like the locals, they stayed away when the cruise ship crowds descended on the beach bar, but it usually quieted down later in the day. Devan would have preferred somewhere more upscale, but she'd humored Nicky when he suggested they go there that evening, since there was something on her mind she wanted to broach with him.

Nicky set the drinks down with a smile. "I ordered some snacks. Sean says the kitchen's not busy, so they won't be long."

Devan replied through gritted teeth. "Great. I thought we were going to The Westin for dinner, but never mind."

Nicky raised an eyebrow. "Is everything okay? You seem kind of tense."

Devan tried to slow her breathing, despite the fact her heart was racing. One, two, three. Her dumb therapist said counting was supposed to calm her down. *Maybe if I count to a thousand*, she thought to herself, *it would work but that would take a long time.* Meanwhile, as she tried to calm herself, Nicky looked at her with a quizzical expression. "It's work," she snapped. "My boss is an incompetent. You really need to get him fired, Nicky."

"Hmm." Nicky lazed back in his chair, raking a hand through his long thick hair. "I'm not sure if I can arrange for the head of Goldstone Private Banking to lose his job. Especially since his father owns the bank."

Devan scowled. "It's ridiculous. People should be employed on merit, not who they know or who they're related to."

"Says the woman whose last three jobs were arranged by me."

"That's different. I have qualifications. It's not my fault if the people I work for feel threatened by my talent," Devan said with a pout.

Nicky took a gulp of his beer. "Are you sure you're not overreactin'? George Town's a small place. Can I make a suggestion?"

"You're going to anyway, so I don't know why you're asking."

"You should probably try and hold down a job for more than a couple of months or you'll run out of options. I'm runnin' outtta' friends who owe me favors." Nicky's eyes bored into her as he spoke, and Devan scowled.

"I don't see why I have to work at all. Has that ever occurred to you?"

Nicky chuckled. At times like this, his upbeat nature was an annoyance to Devan, whose moods blew hot and cold. The fiery temper she had inherited from her Jamaican mother trumped the placid traits handed down from her British father. Growing up, Devan's mother had ruled the roost, and Devan expected to do the same. Except, much to her frustration, with Nicky Luchesse it didn't quite work that way.

"Of course, it has. You'd like to be a kept woman, is that it? I'm not sure I admire a lazy streak in a woman. I thought you were better than that."

Devan batted her eyes, playing for time. The conversation wasn't going how she'd planned. "I'll ignore that comment, Nicky. This is about making your life better, not mine. There's certain advantages to that sort of arrangement that I'm sure you can appreciate."

A waiter brought several dishes of fried fish, chicken, and fries to the table, and Nicky licked his lips. He grinned up at the waiter. "Thanks, Sean." Turning to Devan, he winked. "Time to eat."

Devan watched him devour the snacks and wondered how to get through to him. "I don't think you're taking me seriously, Nicky. I'm only thinking of you."

Nicky washed down a mouthful of chicken with his beer. "Devan, ya' know I'm very fond of ya', right?"

"I should hope so."

"Well, I am. Thing is, I don't like believe in fixin' things that ain't broke. You got yer' life, I got mine. And the time we spend together is…"

Devan held her breath. *Could this get any worse?* she thought to herself.

Nicky seemed to be searching for the right words. "…a bonus!" His face lit up.

She hoped the stab of hurt that hit her in her chest didn't reach her eyes. It wasn't anything she hadn't heard before, but things had been going well between her and Nicky in previous times, and she'd brushed it off. Now, it felt like Nicky was slipping away from her, and she was left clutching at straws.

It took a great deal of effort for Devan to relax her expression and match Nicky's smile. "You're right. Let's make the most of the time we do get to spend together. When did you say your friends are arriving? I'm looking forward to meeting them."

Nicky grabbed a handful of fries. "Saturday." He stuffed them in his mouth and chomped for a few seconds before continuing. "But I shoulda' said, I ain't seen Al for a while, so we gotta' lot to catch up on. Probably best if ya' make other plans. Between that and some other stuff I've got goin' on, Ima not gonna' have much free time for a while. You don't mind, do ya'?" He reached across and patted her hand.

Devan tried not to flinch. "Of course not." Idly, she added, "This wouldn't have anything to do with Lady Gwendolyn Blackwood, would it?"

"Lady who? Not sure what ya' mean." Nicky picked at the food, avoiding looking at her.

"Oh, I think you do," Devan said smoothly. "I'm sure I saw her car leaving your place last week just as I was arriving. It's a vintage Jaguar, isn't it?"

Nicky scratched his head. "Ah, so that's who that was. She of the good works. It was something to do with a charity auction, if I remember. I pledged some money to make her go away." He followed up with a hollow-sounding laugh.

*It could be true,* Devan thought to herself. Lady Blackwood was known to support various charitable causes, even if all that entailed was selling raffle tickets and drinking gin.

The voice inside her head told her to leave it at that. But in her heart, Devan suspected Nicky was lying. She'd been suspicious for a while that Nicky was hiding something from her, and it was time to find out the truth. Only then could she decide how to deal with it. After all, damage control required knowing the extent of the damage.

"It's not the first time I've seen her at your place, you know." Devan said as she studied Nicky's face. "I'm surprised you said you didn't know her."

Nicky shrugged. "What is this, the Spanish Inquisition? Maybe she came around before, I dunno'. This committee, that committee, always askin' for money. I can't tell one posh lady from another." His expression was challenging, and his eyes were telling her to drop the subject if she didn't want to get hurt any further.

Devan didn't need to count to three as suggested by her therapist. She was on her feet in a heartbeat. "Nicky, when you look in the mirror, do you see Richard Nixon staring back at you? Or, maybe it's Bill Clinton. They were both pretty famous for lying about the truth."

She lifted her purse and turned her back, walking out of the bar slowly to show him what he was losing. Only when she was out of sight did the tears start to flow.

*****

By the time she arrived back at the apartment she shared with her younger sister Naomi, Devan's sorrow had flipped to anger. Naomi looked up from where she was studying at the dining room table and closed her books. "What happened? Just the highlights will do."

Devan relayed the condensed version of her conversation with

Nicky, spitting the words out as she went along. "Five years," she said. "Me, Devan Parker, turning down potential suitors because I loved him. I've wasted the prime time of my life on that playboy. How could I be so stupid?"

"You're only twenty-nine," Naomi pointed out. "Hardly past your prime yet."

"That's not the point. Never trust an older man with a ponytail, that's all I can say. I mean, what does he see in Lady Blackwood?" She slumped onto the sofa, its squishy pillows covered in cream linen slipcovers, and thought she might never be able to get up.

"Must be the forbidden fruit effect," Naomi said with a giggle. "Being married is the only thing she has going for her."

"Is that it, do you think? Was I too available?" Devan gazed at the opposite wall, where a spider's web gathered dust in the corner.

"Move over." Naomi sat down beside her. "Does it matter? You always knew it wasn't a conventional relationship. Nicky likes to have his cake and eat it too." She looked pointedly at Devan's bracelet. "And he does buy you nice things. Not to mention finding you a new job every time you get fired. Maybe you shouldn't be so hasty before you consider your options."

Devan stared at her sister. Her voice was slow and steady. "You don't get it. All I ever got from Nicky was just enough crumbs to keep me hungry. It's not about money anymore."

"Isn't it?" Naomi looked confused.

"No. He's overstepped the line in the sand. I've thrown away the best years of my life on that man, but I still have my pride and my dignity."

"The best years of your life so far, Devan. I think when you've slept on it, you'll realize things aren't that bad. Actually, you're better off without him if you ask me." Naomi got up and walked over to the refrigerator. She opened the door and pulled out a bottle of wine.

Devan glared at her. "I don't remember asking you."

Naomi began to pour the wine into two glasses she'd set on the counter. "What are you going to do about it?"

"Remember what happened to Justin Donnelly?"

Naomi handed her a glass of wine and sat down again. "Your ex, Justin Donnelly?"

"That's the one." A slow smile spread across Devan's face.

"You've lost me. I thought he had a fatal accident one day when he was cleaning his gun."

Devan laughed. "Yes, that's what everyone thought."

*Nicky Luchesse has no idea who he's dealing with. I got away with murder once. Who's to say I won't again?* Devan thought to herself as a plan of action started to form in the back of her mind.

# CHAPTER THREE

Benedetto Amato, known as Benny to his friends and foes alike, swore under his breath. "Gino's not going to like this," he muttered to himself, squinting at the computer screen. Benny barely knew the basics of how to use a spreadsheet, and he scratched his head with a sigh. Lifting a pen, he scrawled some numbers on a blank page of a notebook lying on the desk where he was sitting, so he could see if they made more sense that way.

"Gino's not going to like what?" Sam Hayman, Benny's newly recruited assistant said as he entered the shabby office holding a couple of coffees, and handed one to Benny.

"Thanks, kid." Benny took a sip and winced. He looked up and shook his head at Sam. "I thought I told you, more cream? A guy could burn his tongue on that." He handed the mug back to the younger man. "And three sugars, not two. Didn't they teach you how to make coffee in Chicago Heights?"

His face broke into a smile as Sam scurried off. The truth was, Benny would take his coffee any way it came, but he thought Sam may as well learn how to do it right. Following orders was crucial in their line of work. Stupid mistakes had serious consequences. Benny had known a lot of dead people who had learned that lesson the hard way.

Several minutes later Sam said, "Here, boss," and thrust another mug of coffee in front of Benny. "Is that better?"

Benny took a sip and paused while he tasted the coffee. *Not bad. Not bad at all. The kid's learning,* he thought to himself. Aloud, he said, "It'll do," and Sam breathed an audible sigh of relief.

"Listen up," Benny said, pushing his notebook across the desk to Sam, who had taken a seat across from him. "While you were off crunching coffee beans I was crunching some numbers. What do you make of these?"

Sam took one look and his eyes widened. "Gino's going to freak out. He won't pay that much."

Benny rolled his eyes. "Yeah, that's what I've been thinking. Did Nicky mention anything to you about the missing shipment?"

Sam exhaled. "Same as what he told you, that the boat caught fire and all the ganja went up in flames. He sounded pretty upset about it. Said Jevaun's looking for compensation for the boat, as well. It's lucky the crew didn't go up with it."

"Yeah, I'm not so sure Gino's going to be quite so understanding," Benny said. "He's expecting a delivery, and now we can't make it. Gino's going to have to let some people down. You know what that means, right?"

Sam shook his head. "'Afraid I don't, Boss."

Benny leaned across the table and Sam shrank back. "Listen up, kiddo." Benny chuckled. "I'm not going to eat you. The first rule in our kind business is to never let anyone see you're scared, got it?"

Sam gulped. "Yep."

"That's better." Benny rubbed his chin. "Now then, we got ourselves a problem. The way our costs have been going up, there's no way we can pass a price hike on to Gino. Our margins are getting hit every which way. With a shipment missing, we're going to have to make other arrangements to keep Gino happy. That's going to cost us, big time."

Sam looked confused. "Can't you just tell Gino we don't have enough, um, candy? Maybe he can get it somewhere else."

Benny gave Sam a strange look. "You don't get it, do you? That's not how it works." He leaned back his head and roared with laughter until his body shook. When Benny was finished laughing, he turned serious. "The second rule in our kind of business is don't get killed."

Sam, shifting noticeably in his seat, paled.

"Gino don't care what happened to the candy," Benny explained patiently. "A deal's a deal. We already agreed on a price and we agreed on the quantity." He pointed his forefinger at the quaking twenty-something sitting across from him. "You, Sam, need to go find enough candy for us to keep Gino happy when he gets here tomorrow. It's got to be good stuff, you hear me? Try it if you have to. Have some fun on me."

Sam brightened a little. "Sure. What's the budget?"

Benny scribbled a number on a scrap of paper and gave it to Sam.

"No way, Boss." Sam stared across at him, wide-eyed. "There's no way I can get it for that price. Are you crazy?"

*This kid's starting to bug me now,* Benny thought to himself. *He doesn't get how much trouble we're going to be in tomorrow when Gino shows up.* He slammed the table with his fist before standing up abruptly. "Sam, quit snowflaking around. This is serious. Borrow, beg, or steal it if you have to, but don't come back here till you've got what we need. Do I make myself clear?"

"Yep." Sam's head was nodding like a bobbing dashboard toy. "You can count on me, Boss."

With a sinking heart, Benny watched Sam rush out of the room. It was a tough test for any kid, and he suspected Sam wasn't ready for it. He tried to shake the feeling and pulled a cigar out of the top drawer of his desk before sinking back in his chair and lighting it.

As he exhaled a cloud of smoke, visions of a boat load of marijuana going up in flames passed before his eyes, and he punched Nicky's number into the phone.

*****

He had known it was a tall order, but Benny took no pleasure in having been right about Sam. Finding a new assistant to replace Sam was the least of his worries. He let himself into his Lakeshore Drive condominium and shut the door with a quiet click, so as not to wake his wife.

In the kitchen, he opened the refrigerator and pulled out the first thing he saw. As he was biting into a cold chicken drumstick, two arms slid around his neck while he was still looking to see what else he could find to eat. He froze for a second, fear etched on his face, until the scent of a familiar perfume made him relax. Turning around, Benny gave his wife, Lauren, a greasy kiss.

"Ugh," she said, pulling away. She wiped her mouth with the back of her hand. "Next time, kiss me when you're done with the midnight snacks."

Benny munched on the chicken. "You have no idea how happy I am to see you," he said, between bites. "I thought you'd be asleep."

Lauren looked at him with concern. A yoga devotee and holistic health expert, his wife eschewed the cosmetic treatments favored by her middle-aged contemporaries, although she often scolded Benny for giving her more worry lines than she'd like to have.

In the dim light of the open refrigerator door, Benny thought she looked just as beautiful as when he'd married her thirty years earlier. The women who threw themselves at him on his travels weren't for

Benny. He was strictly a one-woman-man. The only woman he looked at was his wife.

"I was worried about you. That's why I stayed up and waited for you." Lauren frowned. "How'd it go with Gino?"

Benny shook his head, and his voice cracked when he eventually spoke. "He's not happy. One of his men shot Sam. The kid's in the hospital."

"Is he going to be alright?"

Benny shrugged. "You know how it goes. Gino said he was teaching him a lesson. I blame myself. I should have just had a word with Gino and told him we messed up. Instead, Sam tried to fix it and look what he got for not getting it right."

Lauren pulled out a stool and sat down at the kitchen counter. "What's Nicky got to say about all of this? He's the one who's supposed to be keeping an eye on things, instead of leaving you to sort it all out. If Gino's started shooting people, things have gotten way out of hand."

"If I could get Nicky on the phone, I'd ask him." Benny's eyes clouded over. "I think he's been smoking too much of the wacky backy himself, if you know what I mean. Island life's gone to his head. Women and boats and weed seem to be the only things on his mind these days. He's so laid back about the Jevaun thing, I'm starting to wonder if he isn't involved in it somehow. Maybe they've cut a side deal. I can sense he's keeping something from me."

He closed the refrigerator door, and the kitchen was bathed in darkness. He heard Lauren giggle from the counter, and he reached out with both arms while his eyes adjusted to the sudden darkness. When he found her, he nuzzled his head into her softness. "No more midnight snacks," he murmured. "Let's go to bed."

Lauren lay sleeping soundly while Benny, wide awake, tossed and turned as the wind whipped up outside. He felt bad Sam had to learn the hard way how not to deal with someone like Gino Marcetti when he was mad, but that was the reality of being in this type of business. The fact Lauren hadn't so much as batted an eye when he'd told her what had happened to Sam showed even she was immune to the process. *Gino was right. Better the kid was taught a lesson now than get hit later,* Benny reasoned to himself. *Anyway, since when did I get so soft?*

The more he thought about Sam, the more Benny couldn't sleep. He tried Nicky's phone number again, but the line went straight to voicemail. *Nicky wouldn't try and rip me off, would he?* Benny wondered. He became more and more agitated and obsessed by the thought.

Lauren stirred beside him, and he gently stroked her silken blond hair. He got up so as not to disturb her. Pulling on a robe, he crept out through the living room and onto the balcony, where he kept a stash of cigars. Smoking helped him think.

He and Nicky had been partners in their import business for years, splitting the profits down the middle after the Jamaican marijuana grower had been paid, and transportation costs and bribes had been taken care of. Nicky organized the shipments locally with Jevaun Henriques, and Benny dealt with the logistics when the cargo arrived at a secret location in the Florida Keys and then got forwarded on to Chicago. According to Nicky, Jevaun had been asking for more money for the last few shipments which was cutting down on their take.

What was bugging Benny, was why Nicky was so calm about it all? Was it really all that weed he'd been smoking, or was there something else going on? Benny realized what had been staring him in the face all along, and his anger started to build.

*Nicky's gone rogue and he's shorting me,* he thought as he fumed. *Lost at sea, my foot. That lying, two faced son-of-a-gun. Let's see if Nicky would like a taste of what Sam got.*

Benny blew smoke rings into the air, and watched the wind carry them away.

*Except it won't be a warning, because Nicky ought to know better. Where Nicky's going, there's no coming back,* Benny thought with a wide smile of satisfaction on his face.

# CHAPTER FOUR

DeeDee sipped her coffee and looked over at Jake's crossword puzzle. Several blank squares remained. "Relax."

He gave her a sideways look. "I thought I was. Relaxing, I mean."

"Five across. The answer to the clue, 'Take things easy' is relax. She pointed at the clue and then looked out the window of the airport lounge, where a plane was taxiing down the runway. "Having that answer in the crossword seems like a good omen, I think," she added with a smile, while Jake filled in the missing letters.

"What does?" Al strode towards them, a small backpack slung over his shoulder. Cassie followed behind, wearing headphones and nodding her head in time with whatever music she was listening to.

"A whole week with nothing to do but chill out." DeeDee beamed up at him. "Did you get Red taken care of?"

Al nodded. "Yeah, they're loadin' him now." He patted his pockets before turning to Cassie with a worried look. "Do you have the boardin' passes, honey? I just want to check where we're seated. We're supposed to be sittin' up front in the plane."

Cassie wheeled her small carry-on bag to a stop beside Al and removed her headphones. "What's that about the boarding passes?"

she asked as she smiled up at him. "I gave them to you."

Everyone stared at Al, who proceeded to pat himself down all over again. "I musta' set 'em down somewhere." He adjusted his sunglasses and grinned. "Back soon, folks. Hopefully I'll find 'em before they call the flight." He checked his watch. "Ten minutes. Plenty of time."

They watched him turn around and retrace his steps through the lounge, muttering to himself. He hadn't gone far before he stopped to greet a woman and they fell into conversation like old friends. DeeDee glanced up at Cassie. "I hope Al finds your boarding passes. He doesn't seem too worried."

Cassie flopped down onto the seat beside DeeDee and gave a light-hearted sigh. "He always does this. Every time we go somewhere, there's a holdup because he's misplaced something. If it's not his phone, it's his passport or his wallet. We've never missed a flight yet, although it's been close. If Al's not racing down the gangway as they're closing the doors on the plane, it's not a proper airport departure. He knows they won't take off without him once the luggage has been loaded onto the aircraft."

Jake chuckled. "That old trick." He paused and cocked an ear. "Sounds like our flight's being called, ladies."

A shout from the other end of the lounge made them turn. "Right on cue," Cassie said, standing up.

Al barreled towards them waving the boarding passes. "Safe in my backpack," he said when he reached their group. "And we got plenty of time to spare for a leisurely stroll to the gate. Shall we?"

He reached for Cassie's carry-on bag and they set off in the direction of the gate.

DeeDee waited for Jake to fold his newspaper and pick up the latest Jack Reacher book he'd bought at the airport book store. "You've got our boarding passes, right?" she asked him.

He gave her a blank stare. "I thought I gave them to you."

DeeDee shook her head, watching Jake frantically begin to search through his pockets. The final call for their flight came over the public address system, and DeeDee was unable to keep a straight face any longer. "I'm kidding," she said, pulling a travel wallet from her carry-on. "We'd better get going."

They headed in the same direction as Al and Cassie, who had waited for them before getting in line.

"I like gettin' on last and sittin' near the front," Al confided to DeeDee, as they held back while everyone else boarded. "Can't be too careful."

She nodded. Anyone who went anywhere with Al was familiar with his habit of checking the safety of his surroundings at all times. She suspected that was one of the reasons he always wore sunglasses, so other people couldn't see his eyes darting around everywhere he went. She'd even seen him check the underbelly of his car for explosives before getting in. It seemed like being retired from the Mob still had its dangers.

When they were settled in their seats, Al closed his eyes and promptly fell asleep during the safety demonstration being conducted by the flight attendants. Cassie placed her headphones in her ears, leaving DeeDee and Jake to admire the view during the takeoff. As the plane leveled off at its cruising altitude, DeeDee swallowed to relieve the pressure that had built up in her ears. With a pop, her hearing normalized, and the sound of the engines came back into focus.

Jake reached for her hand and gave it a gentle squeeze. DeeDee gazed out the window until the view was obscured by a layer of white fluffy clouds, and then they both settled back to read their books. Every now and then Al would snore or grunt, causing DeeDee to giggle. Cassie, with her headphones on, was oblivious to her husband's sound effects.

About an hour into the flight, DeeDee nudged Jake excitedly. "Look," she said, pointing below. "There's Cuba."

Jake leaned across her and looked out the window. It won't be long now," he said. "We'll be landing at Grand Cayman soon. It's half the distance between Miami and Cuba."

DeeDee's eyes remained glued on the bird's-eye-view of Cuba, an island isolated from the world for sixty years. Its stunning coastline was dotted with a string of cays. Even after they'd passed it by, she continued to be mesmerized by the brilliant turquoise blue of the Caribbean Sea, clear with the exception of an occasional boat.

"Ten minutes until landing," the captain announced twenty minutes later.

DeeDee could see Grand Cayman stretched out below, long and thin. At one side, the land curved around a semi-circular bay.

Al stirred. He opened one eye, stretching out his arms. "Do you see the crescent-shaped part of the coastline, DeeDee, on the far end?" he asked with a lazy smile.

She nodded.

"That's Seven Mile Beach. Our little place ain't far from there. The big bay in the middle is the North Sound. See how the water's a lighter blue in there? That's a shallow reef-protected lagoon."

"Wow." Jake's head nestled in close to DeeDee's, craning to see the vibrant coral reef. "The lagoon is huge."

"It's home to a neighborhood of stingrays that gather together as a group on a couple of sandbars at the mouth," Al added. "The locals call it Stingray City. We can take a trip there, and wade through the water up close with 'em. It's only a coupla' feet deep."

Two large cruise ships were moored off the most built-up part of the island, which DeeDee took to be the capital, George Town. She knew from her guidebook that the city was also the site of the ruins of colonial era Fort George. "I can't wait to explore all of it," she said, grinning with excitement as the plane descended towards the airport.

Cassie removed her headphones and joined the conversation. "There are some lovely shops, and as for the cuisine, trust me, DeeDee, you'll think you've died and gone to seafood heaven."

"In that case, there's definitely a lobster with my name on it," Jake said.

The plane hit the runway and the brakes came on, forcing everyone backwards with a jolt. When they reached a stop, Al jumped up and opened the overhead bin as soon as the seatbelt sign was switched off. "Another reason why I like sittin' at the front is that we get to be the first ones off. Ready?"

They all nodded in unison.

"Let's go. Follow me." Al led the way, taking on his host role with great enthusiasm. When they'd cleared Immigration and collected their checked luggage and Red in his wire kennel, Al and Jake wheeled their baggage carts into the main terminal. In the Arrivals hall, a local man was waiting for them, holding a sign saying 'De Duco.'

"DeeDee, Jake, this is Teddy," Al said, before greeting the man with a friendly slap on the back.

Teddy solemnly shook each of their hands in turn, adding a little bow and a smile when he came to Cassie.

"Teddy's wife, Chandice, is our housekeeper," Al explained, "They both look after our place while me and Cassie are gone."

"And Holt," Teddy added.

Red barked.

"That's our other dog here, a small little Husky," Cassie said. "He and Red are great buddies, isn't that right, Red?" She reached through the cage to stroke the Doberman. "Don't worry, big guy, we'll have you out of there real soon."

Teddy led them to a large SUV with just enough room for all of them to squeeze inside along with their luggage. There wasn't enough space for Red's cage, but Al had already made arrangements for it to be stowed at the airport until their return trip. He released Red and took the cage back inside while Jake took Red for a walk around the parking area to stretch the dog's legs and otherwise take care of business.

DeeDee waited with Cassie, who was talking to Teddy. "We'll have lunch at the house today, and we're going out later," Cassie said. "So, don't worry about dinner."

Teddy nodded. "Mr. Nicky called yesterday. He said he'll be around all afternoon, so he'd like you to come over to his place whenever you're ready. He also asked if Mr. Al and Mr. Jake would like to go fishing in the morning, on his Princess boat."

"Princess Leia?" Al had returned, catching the tail end of the conversation. He waved Jake over. "Did ya' hear that, Jake? We should be honored. That vessel's Nicky's prized possession. I've only been on it once, after I got my sea legs, and lemme' tell ya' it's a beaut'."

When everyone, including Red, had gotten in the car, Teddy started the engine and headed towards the exit.

DeeDee shared a smile with Cassie. "In that case, since the men are going fishing, it looks like the two of us are going shopping tomorrow. Whatever these guys catch, we can cook for dinner."

"Deal," Al said.

DeeDee took in the surroundings as the big SUV sped away from the airport. They weaved through the traditional architecture of

George Town, towards the condo complexes and hotels in the Seven Mile Beach area. Just when she thought they were headed for one of the highly-populated developments, Teddy turned down a road that seemed like it was going nowhere.

DeeDee gasped when the ocean and a wide white sandy beach came into view. She was in awe as they drove past several houses tucked behind iron railings and vibrant foliage, all with beach frontage.

"That's Nicky's place," Al said with a nod as they passed the biggest house on the row. "And we're just on down a bit, around this bend." He paused as a black railing came into view. "Here we go."

Teddy pressed a remote control handset as they approached the gates of the residence which swung open without them having to stop.

DeeDee exchanged a look with Jake. Al and Cassie's home may not have been as big as Nicky's, but it certainly wasn't the 'little' place Al had casually led them to believe.

A smiling woman came out to greet them and introduced herself as Chandice. "Please, come in," she said, as Teddy unloaded their luggage. "I'll show you to your room, Mrs. DeeDee and Mr. Jake. Please, follow me."

Chandice led them through an airy hallway with a tall ceiling and up a central staircase. At the top, the landing split in two directions. They followed her along one side and through a heavy wooden door into a sweeping room that reminded DeeDee more of a hotel suite than a guest bedroom. A four-poster bed faced vast windows spanning a sun terrace and overlooking a lush garden with a pool and a gate leading to the beach beyond. At the other side of the room was a sitting area with a sofa and armchairs. Another door led to a bathroom with a double vanity and a rainfall shower.

"If you need anything, please let me know," Chandice said after showing them around the room. "Lunch is ready downstairs whenever you are."

"Thank you, Chandice." DeeDee waited until Chandice had gone before letting out a squeal of delight and planting a kiss on Jake's cheek. "How the other half live, huh?" She laid down on the bed and closed her eyes. "Am I in heaven? This bed is like a giant marshmallow. I don't think I can get up."

She felt Jake tug at her arm. "You're going to have to, sweetheart, because it's lunchtime, and I have a feeling this day is going to keep getting better."

DeeDee sat up and smiled. "Very well. If you insist."

# CHAPTER FIVE

Lady Gwendolyn Blackwood stared at the white plastic pregnancy test stick in her right hand and prayed for a pink line to appear. Or maybe it was blue. Either way, a line was all she wanted to see. She could care less what color it was, as long as it confirmed the pregnancy she wanted so badly.

Her husband, Sir Alec, banged on the bathroom door. "Is everything okay in there?"

Gwendolyn opened the mirrored cabinet above the wash basin and hastily shoved the stick in the cabinet out of sight, behind some toiletries. She didn't want to have another conversation with Alec about her desire to become pregnant. If she was pregnant, she'd cherish the news alone for a while, before deciding what to do next.

"I'll just be a moment, darling." She tried to make her voice light and carefree. Flipping the cabinet door shut, she fixed her wispy blond hair in the mirror, and pinched her cheeks to add some color.

The door handle rattled. "For goodness sake, will you hurry up, woman. I've got to be on the first tee in ten minutes."

Gwendolyn turned the lock on the inside of the door and opened it. Sir Alec, a short burly man with a shock of unruly dark hair and a large mustache, barged past her, unzipping his pants.

"I'll leave you to it," she mumbled, closing the door behind her. Shivering, she pulled her silk robe tight around her slim frame and climbed back into bed. A tray laden with breakfast things sat on the nightstand, and she poured herself a cup of Earl Grey tea, ignoring the porridge, toast, and fresh fruit the maid had prepared.

"Are you ill, my sweet?" Sir Alec said when he came out of the bathroom and sat on the side of the bed, raising his palm to feel her forehead. "Shall I call Dr. Walsh?"

"No!" There was no way she wanted a doctor poking around until she'd confirmed her condition. Seeing Sir Alec's look of confusion, she mustered a smile. "I just feel a little tired, that's all. I'll have a snooze until Marion gets here. I'm going to that charity lunch with her, remember? At the Ritz-Carlton."

Sir Alec's face clouded over. "Don't be getting carried away with the auction like you did last time. We really don't need any more art. Especially not the splashy abstract pieces that look like a spilled bucket of paint. Old Masters are more my thing." He patted her hand and stood up. "Anyway, charity begins at home, and all that. By the way, the Bentley's acting up, so I'll have to take your car."

"That's fine. The keys are in my purse." She gave him a weak smile. "Oh, and Alec?"

"Yes, dear?"

"It needs gas."

Sir Alec rolled his eyes and stomped off, muttering about being late.

*****

Gwendolyn was still in bed when her best friend, Marion Bartlett, threw open the bedroom door several hours later and came barging into the room.

"What do you think you're doing sleepyhead?" Marion exclaimed as she pulled back the bedcovers. "Gwen?" She prodded her friend's shoulder. "Do get up, you lazy thing. I'm not going to a lunch full of old fuddy-duddies without you. There's not enough gin on the island for that."

Gwendolyn grabbed for the covers. "Lemme' sleep. I'm sick."

"Nope." Marion yanked the covers off one more time, and Gwendolyn finally sat up. Marion folded her arms across her chest and said in a sarcastic tone of voice, "You don't look sick to me. More like you're sulking about something. Are you going to tell me what's wrong, or do I have to drag it out of you?"

Gwendolyn got out of bed and stomped into the bathroom. Returning with a plastic stick, she waved it at Marion. "This…this is what's wrong," she said, shoving it in front of Marion's face. "I'm not pregnant, that's what's wrong!"

Marion smirked. "Lucky you, that's all I can say. Try having three kids, and you'd know why I say that. My figure's ruined, my husband's lost interest in me, and all I've got to show for it are three snivelling little brats who think I'm their servant. Is it any wonder I drink to stay sane?"

Gwendolyn half-laughed. "You're the best mother I know, and your children are adorable. Your house might be a little messy, but I bet it's a lot more fun than living in this mausoleum." She stared at the peeling wallpaper on the bedroom walls and shuddered.

The Blackwood residence was hundreds of years old. It may have looked like a fine old estate from the outside, but the interior was another matter. It had fallen into disrepair before Gwendolyn had lived there, and the remodeling work Alec had promised when they'd gotten married had never materialized.

Marion placed her hands on her hips. "You're saying my house is a little messy?" She giggled. "That's a nice way of putting it, because actually it looks like a train wreck, most caused by unruly children.

Now get dressed, m'lady, and you can tell your best friend Marion all about it." She looked around the room. "Got any gin?"

Gwendolyn, heading for the bathroom, looked back over her shoulder and said, "Downstairs, in the great room. Alec keeps a well-stocked bar. That's one of his plus points." Her face crumbled. "Maybe it's his only one, come to think of it."

Marion steered her into the bathroom. "There's nothing a gin and tonic and a chat can't fix. Don't come down until you're looking like a million dollars, got it?"

Gwendolyn sighed.

"Good," Marion said. "You've got five minutes."

When Gwendolyn appeared downstairs a short while later, Marion nodded at the drinks on the side table. The ice in the short crystal glass clinked as Gwendolyn lifted her glass and sat opposite Marion, who was ensconced on the giant Chesterfield sofa, enveloped by pillows that were faded with age.

"Not bad," Marion said. "Eight minutes, and you look a darn sight better than I thought you would. Now, are you going to tell me what this is all about? I thought the whole children subject was closed. Did Alec change his mind?"

"Not exactly." Gwendolyn stared at Marion, whose face flickered with sudden knowledge.

Marion groaned. "You're still seeing Nicky Luchesse, aren't you? Gwen, you're playing with fire. If Alec finds out, he'll go nuts. I can't believe you're even considering this, having two men on hand. Are you that desperate for a baby you don't care who the father is? Need I remind you that your husband made it very clear, before you were married, that he didn't want a family?"

"What about what I want?" Gwendolyn's face hardened. "Let's not forget Alec lied to me and made promises he couldn't keep either." She picked at the threadbare fabric on the arm of her chair. "Look at this place, it's falling to pieces. The furniture isn't even antique, and it should be condemned. Alec wooed me with promises of grandeur, and I'm not ashamed to admit that a life of luxury appealed to me. I didn't get what I signed up for, so why should he?"

Marion stared at her friend. "Where does Nicky fit into all of this? Have you discussed it with him?"

"No, I haven't, but I think Nicky would come around." Gwendolyn's chin jutted out. "A baby might just be the wake-up call he needs to take our relationship to the next level." She hesitated. "I know he wants to be with me, because he's made that clear enough. He already helps me out financially."

Her face flushed, and Marion started to speak. "No, let me finish," Gwendolyn continued. "Nicky knows Alec doesn't have much money, despite my husband's pathetic attempts to keep up appearances. Nicky likes me to have nice things, and to be available to see him when he's free."

"Hmm." Marion raised an eyebrow. "There's a name for that, you know. It's called being a kept woman."

Gwendolyn shifted in her chair under Marion's intense stare. "There's no point in lecturing me, Marion. I know what I'm doing. If I get pregnant by Nicky, he'll make sure that the baby and I are taken care of financially, even if he doesn't want to be involved."

"And Alec?"

"My husband would divorce me in a heartbeat at the scandal that would erupt, which would be a perfect end to a not-so-perfect marriage." Gwendolyn laughed hollowly. "Imagine! The Blackwood family name, tarnished by a trollop. Alec and I are rarely intimate anymore. He's too busy playing with those electronic gadgets of his. So, if a baby were to be in the cards, it's unlikely to be his."

Marion drained her glass. "Oh boy. I think I need another drink.

You?"

Gwendolyn nodded. "Sure. It's not like I have any reason to abstain." She held out her glass to Marion, who walked over to the bar in the corner of the room and set the glasses down.

"Nicky strikes me as someone who likes his independence," Marion said. "He may not be very thrilled to know he was a pawn in this scheme of yours." She lifted a heavy crystal decanter containing gin and pulled out the chunky stopper with a pop. "What if it all backfires? I agree Alec will kick you out, there's no doubt about that. Have you considered what you will do if Nicky dumps you too?" She began to pour, the gin making a splashing sound as it tumbled over the ice cubes in the glasses.

Gwendolyn's eyes narrowed. "Why do I get the impression there's something you're not saying? If the worst happens and I'm left on my own with a baby, I'll manage. That child will never be short of love." A smile spread across her face. "This is silly. It's neither here nor there. I'd be surprised if Nicky doesn't ask me to marry him. It will work out, you'll see."

Marion returned with the drinks and handed one to Gwendolyn. When she sat back down on the Chesterfield, her face turned solemn. "I don't want to see you get hurt, that's all. At your age, conception isn't impossible, but it's not guaranteed either, and it certainly can be risky to your health. Nicky Luchesse isn't the answer to your problems, darling, and I hate to watch you going through this, and deluding yourself into thinking he is."

Gwendolyn set her glass down on the side table with a thud. "I knew it. What the heck is going on, Marion? I didn't know you had anything against Nicky. I thought you liked him. Stop talking in riddles and spit it out."

"Fine." Marion exhaled loudly. "The thing is…you're not the only woman in Nicky's life. I happen to know he's seeing someone else." Her face softened as she watched Gwendolyn's expression crumble. "I'm so sorry, but I think it's better that you hear it now from me rather than when it's too late. Gwen?" She jumped up in horror. "Oh, my goodness, are you alright?"

Gwendolyn had wrapped her arms around herself and was huddled over with her head between her knees, rocking herself back and forth. The wail she omitted was akin to the screeching of a wounded animal. Marion rushed to soothe her and crouched down on the floor at her friend's knees. They stayed like that for some time. Gwendolyn alternated between sobs and rants as Marion watched in silence unable to do much more than simply look at her friend who was clearly racked with emotion.

"Thank you for telling me," Gwendolyn finally said after a while, when there were no more tears left. Her face was stony. "I guess this changes everything," she said in an angry tone of voice.

Marion eased herself up from the floor, her knees creaking. "Do you still want to go to the lunch thing? I totally understand if you don't. We can skip it, and I'll send a check to the committee as a donation." She smiled. "I love spending my husband's money on worthy causes."

"Who is she?" Gwendolyn's voice was pleading. "I need to know, Marion."

Marion sighed. "Devan Parker. She works at the bank where I have an account. I've seen her wrapped around Nicky at Calico Jack's more than once. I would have said something before, if you'd told me you two were still seeing each other. She's a nice person, if it's any consolation."

"It's not. Is she pretty?"

Marion nodded. "Drop dead gorgeous."

"Young?"

"Late twenties."

"Great. I've no chance against a woman not much more than half my age. Anyway, it's not her I'm mad at, it's Nicky. Now I know why he was being so cagey when I tried to pin him down about us spending more time together. He said he couldn't commit due to spending time in Miami and Chicago in connection with his work. Now I know who he was with, on his little trips."

"What are you going to do?"

Gwendolyn rubbed her eyes and took a deep breath. There was only one thing she could do. Never, ever, had she expected to have her hopes and dreams shattered in a blinding flash in an instant. Nicky Luchesse had no regard for anyone but himself. All the lies, all the times he told her he loved her. Did he tell Devan Parker that, too? Gwendolyn decided right then and there she would make Nicky pay for hurting her like this. She would throw a little suffering Devan Parker's way too. A plan began to form in her mind.

*My life has just come crashing down. Let's see how Nicky likes a taste of his own medicine,* she thought to herself.

She stood up and smiled at Marion. "Nicky's not worth my tears. You and I are going to lunch."

# CHAPTER SIX

"More wine, DeeDee?" Al lifted the bottle to top off her glass before DeeDee had even replied.

"Just a little," she said with a smile. "Wine goes straight to my head during the day. I don't want your friend Nicky to think I'm a lush."

Al began to pour, stopping when her glass was half-full. "No chance. I've known many a lush in my time, an' you sure ain't one of 'em." He turned to his left and began to refill Cassie's glass. "My wife, on the other hand…"

Cassie threw him an eye-roll, waiting until he was done. "Says the man who could drink an elephant under the table," she said, raising the glass to her lips and taking a sip. "I'm practically a teetotaler, holidays excepted. I'm only having another glass because DeeDee and I are going to laze around here all afternoon and work off lunch with a few laps in the pool. If you and Jake want to go explore the island, go right ahead. You won't hear any complaints from us."

"I second that," DeeDee said. "Although it will take more than a few laps to work off that lunch. Chandice really pulled out all the stops."

"If I'm not mistaken, DeeDee's little notebook should be coming out any second now," Jake said, while DeeDee began to rummage in her purse.

"Only because I want to ask Chandice what was in the seafood quiche," DeeDee said, setting a small leather-bound journal and a pencil on the table. Her eyes twinkled. "Jake knows every time we try a new dish when we're out somewhere, I see it as a recipe opportunity for Deelish. I've been sending them on to Susie while we've been away."

During the time she and Jake had been living temporarily in Connecticut, her assistant, Susie, had been in charge of running her catering business back on Bainbridge Island. Despite DeeDee's absence, Deelish had continued to grow, especially since she'd cut Susie in on a slice of the profits.

It had been Jake's idea, with the result that the extra money and responsibility she'd given Susie had been dwarfed by the overall jump in revenue. DeeDee was a sharp businesswoman, and as well as genuinely liking Susie, she knew it was in her best interests to make sure Susie was well looked after financially.

"Speaking of recipes, we love your cookbook," Jake said to Cassie. "Or should I say DeeDee loves preparing the dishes, and I love eating them." Holt, the house's resident Husky, wandered over to the table, and Jake reached down to stroke his black silken coat.

"I can't really take the credit for that," Cassie said. "The recipes are for some of my favorite dishes I reviewed for my Food Spy column in The Seattle Times. All I did was persuade a few of the chefs from Seattle's top restaurants to allow them to be published for a good cause." She looked wistfully into the distance before continuing. "A lot of the amazing photos were taken by my friend Toni Adams, who was sadly murdered before the book was finished. Her sister, Hillary, stepped in and made sure the remaining photos were of the same high quality. It really was food porn at its finest. The publishers waived their fee and all of the proceeds are going to the Seattle Foundation."

"It's so sad about Toni," DeeDee said. "But what a wonderful legacy. I'm looking forward to meeting Hillary when we get back. Is it true she's dating Rob?"

Al cleared his throat. "Time for us to get outta' here, Jake," he said, standing up. "All this talk about who's friendly with who is too much information, don'tcha think? Especially where Rob's concerned. Poor guy's ears are probably burnin'."

Jake nodded, and finished his beer in two gulps. "Yep. I think I know what's coming next. We'll leave you two to talk about our employees in peace and quiet, ladies, with no interference or snide comments from us." He leaned over and kissed DeeDee before getting up and joining Al.

DeeDee and Cassie watched the two men meander down the path leading towards the ocean before continuing their conversation.

"I get it," Cassie said with a tinkle of laughter. "The fact that the two men working for Al and Jake in their private investigation business are dating people close to us is a touchy subject. Al doesn't think he should treat them any differently at work just because we see them socially. Ever since Luke's been dating my daughter Briana, he's become more like one of the family."

DeeDee thought for a second. "Al's a big softie, as we both know. I guess maybe he doesn't want to lose his edge at work if Rob and Luke see that side of him. He likes coming across as big and scary." She glanced at Holt, who was staring at her from a distance with shiny, wary eyes. "Kind of like Holt, although he's not that big, but he's kind of scary."

Cassie slapped her leg, and Holt came bounding over. "Holt's a softie too," she said, "if you can see past his teeth."

"I can," DeeDee said, thinking of her husky dog, Balto, who was a big fluffy bundle of fun. She couldn't imagine playing Balto's favorite game, rabbit frisbee, with Holt. *Unless it's a real rabbit, then he might be interested,* she thought to herself.

"Have Briana and Luke ever made a trip here to the Caymans?" DeeDee asked. "This house is beyond amazing. I'm sure they'd enjoy staying here."

"I know," Cassie said. "Al and I both wish we could spend more time here, but it's hard to get away. Briana and Luke are even busier than we are. Briana won't commit to a vacation because she's concerned she'll miss a work opportunity. She's still looking for a bigger place, so she's saving every penny she can. We've offered to help her out, but she won't hear of it."

"My darling children had no such qualms when I gave them money from my divorce settlement," DeeDee said. "But I'm glad how it turned out, since it meant when I met Jake we started with a clean slate."

Cassie poured them both some water. "We were lucky, you with Jake and me with Al. A year ago, I was grieving a murdered husband, and you were struggling to move on from your divorce. Look at us now—both in the middle of love's not-so-young dream. Who'd have thunk it could happen to a couple of older women, huh?"

DeeDee raised her glass. "I'll drink to that. Love, I mean, not the old bit." A flock of colorful birds passing overhead caused her to look up. "Wow. I'm going to have to keep my camera on hand as well as my notebook while we're here. I have no idea what those beautiful creatures are."

"Al might know." Cassie squinted in the sunlight, before reaching for her sunglasses. "He's really into nature. It was one of the things that surprised me when I got to know him, especially since he grew up in Chicago. I think that's why he likes it here so much. It's the other extreme of what he was exposed to for most of his life."

"How long has he owned this place?" DeeDee asked as she looked around. She could see that several additions had been made to the structure, although they were consistent with the style of the original dwelling.

"A long time, from what I can gather," Cassie said as she followed DeeDee's gaze. "It started out as a bit of a hideout, away from whatever trouble Al and Vinny found themselves in over the years. At first, it was only a small one-story building. When Al got a bit more money here and there, he acquired more land to extend the property so he could add on to the house. He always planned on living here someday. Still does, I think. He likes it that Nicky lives a few doors down. They're great buddies."

DeeDee groaned. "Please don't move to the Caymans just yet. I was looking forward to us spending more time together when Jake and I get back to Bainbridge. You only just moved there."

"Oh, don't worry. It won't be for a while. Al's in his glory working again, and I love my job at the paper. In fact, it could hardly be called work. Eating out and getting paid for it so I can write my food column for the Seattle Times is my idea of a dream come true."

"You and me both. Have you met Nicky before?"

Cassie nodded, and stifled a yawn. "We had him over for dinner the last time we were here. Nice guy, if a bit…iffy, is the only way I could describe him. I found him guarded, but maybe that's to be expected, considering his occupation. Not that we discussed it, of course. And Al said he has a girlfriend, but Nicky didn't bring her along or mention her once."

"I wonder if she'll be there when we go to his house. In any case, I'm looking forward to meeting Nicky." DeeDee was fascinated by the underworld Al had once inhabited, even though she didn't condone it. Like Jake, she would rather not know the details, but she'd never met a smuggler before nor was she likely to again. For that reason, she wanted to have her wits about her. "Do you mind if I take a little nap before we go out? I think the wine has gotten to me after all. You've got me yawning, and I'm about to fall asleep."

"Sure. Go on up to your room, and I'll knock on your door when the men get back. Knowing Al, they've probably made their way to Calico Jack's, so they might be a while."

DeeDee was already on her feet, looking forward to having the marshmallow bed all to herself, at least for a couple of hours

# CHAPTER SEVEN

Sir Alec Blackwood strode to the front of the line of golf carts and put his clubs in the back of the cart. "Sorry I'm late, Freddie," he said, climbing in beside a portly man tapping a gaming device with his thumbs. Alec wasn't thin either, so it was a tight squeeze. "Car trouble." Besides needing gas, Gwen had neglected to tell him about the loud noise her Jaguar was making. Despite his limited knowledge of cars, he had decided it was caused by a hole in the muffler that would require a trip to the repair shop.

Freddie Jackson looked up with a raised eyebrow. "I heard you arrive," he said. "As did everyone else at the Ritz-Carlton Golf Club. Might be time to trade in those old cars of yours for newer models, old chap." He grinned, revealing yellowed teeth. "Like I did with my last wife. Speaking of which, how's your divine better half?"

"Fine, fine. Let's get going, shall we? We're holding up the line."

Freddie grunted, and put away the gaming device. "Great little toy, that thingy-ma-jig," he said, referring to the gaming device. "Better than the last one you gave me. How's business these days, or is that a touchy subject as well?"

Alec's business, Toyz for Boyz, distributed his own brand of portable gaming devices, remote control cars, helicopters, and virtual reality headsets marketed to adult kids with high net incomes. "That's one way of putting it," he said with a heavy sigh.

The golf cart creaked under their combined weight as Freddie drove towards the first tee box with its breathtaking view of the North Sound. "What's the problem? You know what you tell me won't go any further."

As well as being Alec's regular golf partner, Freddie was also his lawyer, and had been a trusted friend of the Blackwood family for as long as Alec could remember. As far as he knew, the connection between the Blackwoods and the Jacksons went back several generations to when Alec's ancestors, wealthy British landowners, settled in the Caymans. Their fortune had been diluted over the years, but the Blackwood family name still commanded respect.

Freddie stopped the golf cart at the first tee. They climbed out and Alec proceeded to tee up his golf ball.

"Our friends from the East, that's what the problem is," Alec said, taking a couple of practise swings. "The Chinese manufacturers have copied our product line, moved into the distribution business, and are undercutting our prices. They're flooding Amazon and eBay with the same items we're trying to sell through high-end channels.

"Of course, they don't have the Toyz for Boyz branding, but consumers are becoming a lot more savvy. People are buying based solely on price rather than the name on the box. We're having to cut our margins to practically nothing just to keep our inventory moving." He straightened his arms, swung his club, and hit the ball with a loud crack. For a small man, he was strong, and the ball shot down the fairway.

Freddie squinted up at the sky, following the ball's trajectory. "Nice drive, old chap. The breeze is up. You were lucky to miss the water." The picturesque course was deceiving to the uninitiated player, the wind being the main problem.

Freddie then stepped up to the tee and drove his ball past Alec's with a smug smile. "Have you got much financial exposure?"

Alec's pride prevented him from telling Freddie just how much trouble he was in financially, although he suspected Freddie had a fair idea. After they got back in the golf cart, they trundled off towards their balls, and Alec deliberately kept his response vague. "Let's just say I'm hoping to make the holiday toy bestseller list with our latest product. I'm testing it at the moment. I think it could be huge."

"Glad to hear it," Freddie said as he chipped his ball onto the green. His smile turned to a groan as the ball rolled past the pin and off the other side of the green into a bunker.

It was Alec's turn to grin when his own ball landed two feet from the pin. His mood improved as Freddie took several shots to get out of the bunker, while Alec finished the first hole with a par. As the game progressed, his good form continued until the conversation turned personal.

"Sarah-Jane said she saw Gwen at Dr. Umansky's office the other day," Freddie said casually, marking his score card after the fifth hole. "I didn't realize you two were... you know. Trying, I mean."

Alec froze. Dr. Umansky was the fertility doctor Gwen had tried to persuade him to visit a while back, when she had first started her campaign to change his mind about starting a family. Alec had flatly refused. There was no point wasting money on that futile exercise. He hadn't elaborated on his reasons to Gwen and had considered the subject closed. "We're not."

"Forgive me, I've spoken out of turn." Freddie appeared genuinely flummoxed, and his color heightened. He laughed nervously. "I'm not keen on the idea myself, what with three grown-up children already. But my new wife is set on the idea, and I kind of promised. It's fun trying, at least."

A wave of guilt flooded over Alec when he thought of his beloved Gwen and how much she longed for a baby. He would do anything to keep her happy, except that.

"It's something we discussed before we married," Alec said with a heavy heart. "I told Gwen it wasn't for me, and I thought she'd accepted that." He cringed under Freddie's sympathetic gaze.

"It turns out she'd been hoping to change my mind. Now she's running out of time, and that's probably why she went to see Dr. Umanksy. However, I wasn't aware of her visit." *What sort of a husband does that make me?* he thought to himself. His shoulders sagged as he walked back to the cart.

Freddie was silent until they arrived at the next tee. "What's your aversion to children?" he asked as they selected their clubs.

"You knew my parents before they died," Alec said. "They weren't exactly Parents of The Year material. Maybe I'm afraid I'll turn out the same." Just thinking of his childhood brought up mixed love-hate feelings in Alec. He had vague memories of being presented to his parents at a young age by his nanny before bedtime. His mother smelled of expensive face powder and perfume, his father of cigars and alcohol.

After he was sent to an English boarding school at the age of four, he only saw his parents during the holidays. They remained strangers to him right up to the time they died. For Alec, the fact that he was an only child carried a sense of shame. It could only mean one thing, that he was such a disappointment to his parents they couldn't bring themselves to have another.

"No reason to think that, my man. You turned out all right in the end. Any children of yours would love all the electronic games and gadgets you have around the house, eh?"

Alec shook his head. "I'd rather teach my sons to play cricket or shoot, to tell you the truth."

"There you go." Freddie looked pleased with himself. "That sounds like as good a plan as any. Maybe you should reconsider."

Alec replied with an apologetic shrug. "I don't think so. I was never all that good at cricket anyway. The thing is…" He wanted the ground to swallow him up, but he felt like he owed Freddie an explanation. Or was it an excuse? The words tumbled out. "I had a vasectomy years ago. Gwen doesn't know."

"I see. That's a tricky one." Freddie waved down the drinks cart that was approaching. "Never too early for a Bloody Mary. What do you say, old sport?"

Alec didn't say anything and nodded.

Freddie waved the players behind them through, and they sat for a while in the cart which Freddie had parked off to the side of the cart path.

"You could always get the vasectomy reversed," Freddie said at last. "If it means that much to Gwen."

"Do you think I haven't thought of that?" Alec winced. "It was bad enough the first time. I'm not sure if I could go through that again. In the meantime, I feel so guilty for deceiving Gwen that I wait until she's asleep most nights before coming to bed."

The problem was, he'd seen the empty pregnancy test stick in the bathroom that morning, where Gwen had tried to hide it. He didn't need to look at the plastic stick to know the result was negative. Or was it? The pounding in his chest forced him to face up to the truth of what he had pushed to the back of his mind when he was rushing out to meet Freddie earlier. He had just returned from a business trip after being in China for several weeks. Why was Gwen taking the test at all?

"I think Gwen is seeing someone else," Alec said dully, staring at an iguana creeping across the fairway.

"Nicky Luchesse, by any chance?"

Alec turned to Freddie. "You knew? They have a history from a while back, but I thought it was over. I never said anything, in case Gwen left me for him."

"No, just a guess. It's a small island. Word gets around. As does Nicky, might I add."

Alec drained his Bloody Mary. "He's an arrogant low-life. Thinks he's above the law, as well. It's a shame the authorities don't take a closer look into his business interests, to find out where his money really comes from. Because there's no way those laundromats he owns can afford him the kind of lifestyle he leads."

Freddie turned to him. "I hate to say this, but what if..." He cleared his throat. "How do you feel about bringing up some other man's child? Because that's what's going to happen, if Gwen gets pregnant. Either that or she leaves you, of course."

"I couldn't live with a child in the house, knowing it's not mine," Alec said. "I would have to divorce her, if she didn't divorce me first. Either way, it's a mess."

"I'll say. You'd have to sell the house to pay her off."

Freddie hadn't said anything Alec didn't already know. He loved his wife, but this was a matter of honor. Upholding the family name was paramount in Alec's breeding. The Blackwood mansion and the land it occupied had been in the family for several hundred years and was the only thing of value Alec currently owned.

Even without a direct heir, when he died the estate would be bequeathed to Blackwood relatives in England. He had already received a couple of offers from wealthy investors looking for prime real estate on the island and knew its value ran to millions of dollars. If he had to pay off Gwen it would most likely mean that the grand old house would be razed to make way for a glitzy modern development.

"Not happening. My parents would turn over in their graves." Alec chuckled at the irony of his desire to uphold the legacy of the parents who had never showed him any love.

"Chin up old chap," Freddie said, swinging the golf cart back onto the cart path. "I'm sure you'll think of something."

Alec's mood didn't lift for the rest of the round, and he was unconcerned that Freddie had trounced him. He was glad the Ritz-Carlton course only had nine holes, because a daring plan was forming in his mind, and he needed to get away to focus on whether he could pull it off.

He couldn't let Gwen divorce him any more than he could live with another man's baby. That left him no alternative. He would have to make sure Gwen stopped seeing Nicky Luchesse once and for all. With Nicky permanently out of the picture, maybe he could get his marriage back on track once and for all.

# CHAPTER EIGHT

"Where did you and Jake go?" Cassie asked Al when he stepped out of the shower.

Al wrapped a towel around his waist and slapped his belly, one of his little quirks she had become accustomed to during their marriage. "We walked along Seven Mile Beach. Not the whole stretch, just for a ways."

"As far as Calico Jack's, by any chance?"

Al considered her question before reaching for his toothbrush. "Mighta' stopped in for a cold one. Jake was askin' about wreck divin'. He's interested in takin' a trip out to explore the Kittiwake."

Cassie knew from her previous visits to the island with Al that the decommissioned US navy submarine, USS Kittiwake, was situated just eight hundred yards off the shore of Seven Mile Beach. Donated by the US government to Grand Cayman and sunk in 2011, it created an artificial reef which has since become one of the most famous diving spots in the world.

"Jake was able to tell me more about the vessel's history, even though his background's in the Marines, rather than the Navy," Al went on. "Here's an interestin' fact. Did ya' know it was the Kittiwake and her crew that recovered the black box of the

Challenger on the floor of the Atlantic after the space shuttle disaster in the eighties? Jake has advanced rescue diver certification, so he can go down as far as all five decks. Got me to thinkin'."

Cassie stared at Al in the mirror. "Whenever you say that I get worried. Is this going where I think it is? Please don't tell me you're going to try roping Jake into one of your shady plans. I'm pretty sure he won't go for it."

"Shady, moi?" Al let out a hearty laugh. "This one's all on the level. Well, except it's underwater."

Cassie looked on while Al brushed his teeth. He'd told her before about his and Nicky's plan to recover sunken treasure, but she'd never paid much attention. Now she realized she should have known better than to assume it was just another one of his harebrained ideas. As far as Al was concerned, the word impossible was simply not in the dictionary.

Al rinsed his mouth and spit into the basin. "Me an' Nicky could do with an experienced diver on our team. I'm surprised I never thought of it earlier. I told Jake we'd show him the maritime maps at Nicky's place later on. He's got some in the hallway, but the most important one is pinned up on the wall in his office."

"Hmm. X marks the spot, right?" Cassie said as she tried to keep a straight face. It was all coming back to her—the story about the Grand Cayman gold rush which had ensued after a pair of lucky snorkelers found a gold cross encrusted with emeralds just off Seven Mile Beach. The American couple were on vacation at the time and decided to rent some air tanks to see what else they could find in the same area. By the end of their trip they'd pulled up a thirteen-foot gold chain, a platinum bar, and three hundred pounds of silver objects.

Any other loot from that wreck had long since been plundered, but the story had clearly planted seeds of an idea in Al's mind. For the past couple of years, he and Nicky had been studying naval history books going as far back as the time of Christopher Columbus for ships lost in the Caribbean and their charted routes.

Hurricanes, storms, and squalls ravaged the waters of the Caribbean, and perilous rocky reefs hiding just below the surface of the water had been known to tear a hull open causing a galleon to sink in minutes. Strong winds at night could push a ship into any number of hazards from sand bars and reefs to the rocky shore itself.

"Way I look at it," Al explained to her, "there's no shortage of ways for a ship to meet with an untimely end. When ya' think about it like that, it's surprisin' we ain't findin' a whole lot more treasure while lookin' around down there, don'tcha think?" He was convinced there was plenty more to be had for the taking, if he and Nicky could be the first to find it. What had started out as his 'Retirement Project' had turned into his 'Vacation Project' ever since he'd abandoned his retirement and started working with Jake.

"There's more than one X on the map we've put together," Al said, turning to Cassie. "But we're narrowin' it down. Problem I always had was my sea legs, or lack of 'em. Now that I got that under control, with the range of Nicky's boats and Jake's divin' experience, I reckon we could start explorin'." His eyes were dancing. "Might jes' do it this week, whaddya' think?"

Al's enthusiasm melted Cassie's heart. It sounded innocent enough. If Jake agreed and it made Al happy, she was willing to play along. "Just one question," she said, raking a comb through her hair. "If you do find anything, what are the laws about keeping it?"

"Sheesh. That's a no-brainer. Only law I go by is the law of Finders Keepers," Al replied. He walked into the bedroom, and Cassie could hear him whistling to himself while she finished getting ready.

She applied some lipstick and smoothed down her dress before going back into the bedroom. Al was waiting by the window, wearing jeans and a polo shirt. Her heart skipped a beat as he turned and flashed her a million-dollar smile, and she went over to kiss him.

"What was that for?" he murmured, smoothing her hair after their kiss.

"Nothing," she smiled up at him, half of her wishing they weren't going out. "Just because I love you."

He reached for her hand. "Love ya' more."

*****

"There you are." DeeDee looked up as Al and Cassie entered the garden through the open doors at the back of the house. The sun was fading, and DeeDee had a lightweight sweater slung around her shoulders. Cassie had warned her about the cool evenings this time of year, and the wind that could pick up in an instant. "Jake and I just finished his crossword puzzle. I guess that means we're officially ready to go, if you are."

"Sure thing." Al started to lead the way down the garden path, but Cassie called him back.

"We should go the front way, Al. It's rocky and slippery along the shoreline between here and Nicky's place."

Al stopped, and did an about-turn. "Good point. Plus, it's polite to arrive at someone's front door instead of creepin' through their yard an' comin' in the back way. Wouldn't want to catch Nicky unawares, in case he's up to no good." He chuckled. "Just kiddin'," he said, addressing DeeDee and Jake. "Don't want to make him out to be worse than he really is."

DeeDee glanced at Jake. The more she heard about Nicky, the more fascinated she was to meet him.

It was a short walk down the street to Nicky's home, which was newer than Al's. Al explained Nicky had built on the land several years before, after moving from the east end of the island. Apparently, he needed a property with access to water deep enough to moor his boats, although there wasn't enough room for all of them. The others were kept either in dry storage or at a private marina near George Town, depending on which ones he was currently using.

"There's no sand at the back of Nicky's," Al said, striding towards the imposing gates at the entrance to Nicky's home. "The beach just about finishes at my place, at the bend in the coastline. Nicky's garden runs straight to a jetty leading over the rocks to the water, where he can dock a coupla' boats."

"What about security?" Jake asked. "I noticed you didn't lock any doors when we left your place, just the gates."

"That's true," Al said. "But that's cuz' I know ain't no one gonna' mess with Holt or Red while we're gone. Nicky has security cameras, although they're not always switched on."

"Why's that?" DeeDee was confused. "What's the point of someone having security cameras if they don't use them?"

"Maybe he don't want certain things on camera," Al said, pressing the buzzer on the gates. "Things that can come back to bite ya' if the wrong person sees them."

"That makes sense, I guess." DeeDee said as she exchanged a questioning look with Jake. She began to wonder what they were getting themselves into.

After a delay in the gates being opened, Al pressed the buzzer again. "That's strange." He checked his watch. "Nicky said we could come over any time. Maybe we're too early, and he's still getting ready." He punched several numbers into the keypad, and the gates started to creak open. "Lucky I know the code, huh?"

DeeDee hesitated. "Are you sure Nicky will be okay with us just walking in? What if he's…um, busy like you said?"

Al leaned his head back and roared.

"DeeDee, don't pay any notice to Al," Cassie said. "He's messing with you. Nicky and Al are in and out of each other's homes all the time. From what I know of him, Nicky's very informal and won't mind at all. Like Al said, he's probably just in the shower."

DeeDee looked at Jake, who mouthed a silent 'relax'. She smiled at the reference to the crossword clue from earlier. Jake was right, she was being uptight about nothing. There was no rational reason for the tense feeling that had just come over her. Just like the puzzle clue, she decided she needed to "take things easy."

When no one answered the front door, Al pulled out his phone and pointed it at the door, pressing an icon on the screen. There was a click, and Al stepped forward and opened the door to the house. "Neat, huh?" He grinned. "It's an app. Keys are soon gonna' be a thing of the past. Come on in, folks. Ima gonna' find Nicky." He wandered off to the back of the house, followed by Cassie.

Waiting in the hallway, DeeDee admired Nicky's taste in art with a discerning eye. For a house that was so easy to gain entrance to, there were many rare pieces of art on display, including early works by Morris Graves and Kenneth Callahan. They were both artists who DeeDee knew from her time volunteering as a docent at the Seattle Art Museum. Their paintings were very well-known and commanded premium prices at auction. She was surprised Nicky would have their works here on display in the Caribbean.

"What's that?" she said, walking over to where Jake was viewing an old-fashioned framed map. "It's a nautical chart," he said, "hundreds of years old. Apparently, it's a hobby of sorts that Nicky and Al both enjoy. Al wants to tell me more about it later. He was quite mysterious about the details, but it sounds interesting."

Cassie and Al appeared, and Al headed up the staircase.

"Nicky's not downstairs," Cassie said, "but the food's all laid out in the kitchen waiting to go in the oven, so he can't be far away. Al suggested we go outside, and once he finds Nicky they'll come and join us."

DeeDee and Jake followed her through the doorway of what turned out to be the great room. Ceiling to floor windows covered the entire side of the house that overlooked the garden, where a riot of color greeted them. The rolling lawn sloped down towards the sea, the boundary of the property bordered by banana trees. At the end was a low wooden gate, which DeeDee presumed led to the jetty.

They had just stepped onto the grass when Al's shouts could be heard from upstairs. "Nicky! Nicky, Ima comin'."

Moments later, Al came running out of the house onto the lawn. "Jake, follow me," he said, breathless, as he raced towards the gate. "DeeDee, Cassie, don't move. Stay where ya' are."

Jake fell into step alongside Al, and they both rushed towards whatever it was that had caused Al to come running outside on high alert.

DeeDee felt the knot in her stomach tighten. The only time she ever got that feeling was when there had been a murder. A sideways glance at Cassie, whose face was etched with concern, only heightened DeeDee's sense of dread at what the men would find.

*Surely not*, DeeDee thought to herself. *Not again.*

# CHAPTER NINE

Jevaun Henriques stretched out on the lounge at the side of his swimming pool, where three of his younger children were playing in the water.

"Don't splash so much," he called out, placing a fat reefer between his lips. "Daddy doesn't want to get wet." He reached for his pocket lighter just as his phone began to buzz. At the same moment his girlfriend, Ella, came running out of the house with a toddler on her hip and a face looking like a thundercloud.

"Not in front of the children," she yelled, grabbing the joint from his mouth, and scrunching it into tiny pieces in her free hand. Her voice became a hiss, her chin jutting out as she spoke. "We talked about this. I thought you agreed not to get high in front of the little ones."

The children in the water giggled. "What's getting high, mommy?" the little five year old girl with pigtails asked. Her older brother whispered something in her ear and swam off, laughing.

"Never mind, darling," Ella said, giving Jevaun a dirty look. She motioned towards the phone on the table. "Aren't you going to take that call?"

Glancing at the screen, Jevaun rolled his eyes and laid back on the lounge, hands behind his head. "Nope. It's Bob, Nicky Luchesse's main man that takes care of his boats. I can't have that conversation without some help, if you know what I mean." He looked pointedly at the crumbled mess of weed and cigarette paper in Ella's hand. "Here, give me the baby," he said, sitting up and reaching out his arms.

Ella scowled as she handed over the child before walking to the trash bin in the corner of the yard and disposing of Jevaun's ill-fated joint. She returned with a worried look on her face and stood at the edge of the pool, where the little girl was sputtering. "Don't hold your sister's head under the water, Brant. Are you trying to kill her?"

Brant, a skinny eight-year-old, flailed his arms in the air and gave a whoop before diving on top of his sibling again, who squealed in delight.

Ella turned to Jevaun. Even after four children, she looked younger than her thirty years. Her perfect figure was silhouetted against the wall of the poolhouse, and her flawless cappucino-colored skin glowed in the afternoon heat. Jevaun would have married her if it weren't for his wife who lived in the same compound, but in a separate accommodation.

Their adult children from the marriage had moved away. Another former girlfriend, along with the two teenage children she shared with Jevaun, also had their own private quarters on the grounds. Jevaun and Ella and their little ones lived in the main house. Jevaun was still on good terms with all of his baby's mamas to the point of staying overnight with them in turn, much to Ella's dismay. She sat on the edge of Jevaun's lounge, where he was bouncing the baby on his knee. "I thought you said the Nicky problem had gone away."

"Well, it hasn't." Jevaun sighed. "I'd been hoping it might blow over. But Nicky won't let it go. I think he's been taking the heat from his partner in Chicago." He could feel his heart pounding in his chest and kissed his baby son's forehead before handing him back to Ella.

*Twenty kilos of cannabis with a street value of around two million dollars.*

*One fishing boat burned at sea. Was I really so stupid to think Nicky would fall for a ruse like that?* he thought to himself.

What started out as an easygoing business arrangement between Jevaun and Nicky had soured over the past few months. "You're getting greedy," Nicky had told him when Jevaun first broached the subject of raising his prices. "And we have a deal. That's the end of it."

But Jevaun wasn't happy, and that wasn't the end of it as far as he was concerned. He'd always had a master plan, ever since the first time he had taken the thirty-minute plane ride from Jamaica to Grand Cayman when he was a thirteen-year old boy. He never forgot the feeling he had that day.

Jealousy was something he'd never experienced before then, because the poverty he grew up in was no different than that of his neighbors. The son of a farmer, he had food, clothing and his childhood was a happy one. It was only when he witnessed the wealth of both the Grand Cayman residents and the cruise ship tourists who invaded the island a couple of times a week that he realized what he was missing out on. From that moment on, all Jevaun wanted was to be rich. The only commodity he could easily get his hands on that rich people wanted was cannabis. And so, it began.

He'd started small, growing his own cannabis plants on a remote part of his father's land, and convincing some school friends to grow more and sell him their crops. It was easy enough to make the trip to Grand Cayman and sell it to the tourists, through a few contacts he built up over the years. When Jevaun's father died and Jevaun inherited his farm, he started expanding his operations. That's when he came to the attention of the big boys.

In the end it was Nicky Luchesse's offer that was the most attractive. Nicky already had a couple of suppliers he bought cannabis from and had been smuggling it into Miami on tourist boats for a while. But that was way too risky to be sustainable for very long. To avoid detection, it was necessary to keep the quantities tiny, and the same traveler couldn't make the trip too often without arousing suspicion. The more people that were involved, the more people talked, meaning there were a lot of palms to grease. The risks far outweighed the reward.

"I've got a proposal for you," Nicky said one day after Jevaun had been supplying him for a year or so. "I want to increase the order, if you can arrange a private shipment." When Nicky told him the quantities he had in mind, Jevaun assured him shipping would be no problem. Doing the math in his head, he calculated he would easily recoup the cost of a fishing boat with the range to make the trip to Miami via Cuba. They shook on it, and so began a lucrative arrangement for both parties which lasted several years.

The more Jevaun's wealth grew, the more his expenses expanded. It had been a proud day when he'd moved into the large waterfront unit on Grand Cayman, which he later remodeled and added to over time. His insatiable eye for women led to the unusual family living arrangements, and when the children were young there was enough money to keep everyone happy. But lately, his finances had been somewhat stretched.

The costs he incurred for two children attending college in the United States plus another five at the local international private schools and kindergarten were eye-popping. And the little guy on Ella's hip would be adding to the bill soon enough. Jevaun's wife and his two girlfriends charged everything to his credit cards, leaving him with a major cash flow problem and sleepless nights that were only eased by smoking his own weed. He'd tried to convince himself it was a short-term problem that would resolve itself, but things had steadily drifted from bad to worse.

That's when he'd told Nicky he was raising his prices, but Nicky wouldn't bite. Jevaun had started by skimming some of the cargo on a few shipments so the final delivery was short. But it wasn't enough to meet his financial requirements. With mounting bills and the prepayment from Nicky for the outstanding shipment already spent, Jevaun had panicked. Just thinking about it brought out beads of sweat on his forehead.

Ella frowned. "Maybe you could repay the money. Tell him it was a terrible mistake. I'm sure he'd appreciate your honesty."

"It's too late for that." Jevaun wiped his brow. "I'm backed into a corner. He was already suspicious when I told him the shipment got lost, so I arranged for the boat to be burned off the coast of Cuba. That way, the Coast Guard's report confirms the story."

"Are you crazy?" Ella's eyes widened. "You set fire to a perfectly good boat for nothing? I hope the insurance company doesn't sue you for fraud."

"Now who's crazy?" Jevaun's voice was a whisper as he leaned in close to Ella, so as not to be overheard by the children in the pool. "The boat was never insured since I needed to keep it under the radar, so to speak. I thought the fact that I was out-of-pocket too as a result of the incident would be more convincing. Of course, I asked Nicky to cover the cost of a new boat, but he flat-out refused." He scratched his head. "If only he'd leave it at that."

"Where's the…candy as you call it?"

"I want candy, mommy," called her daughter from the side of the pool.

"Somewhere safe, in Cuba." Jevaun's eyes lit up. "That's two million dollars we've got coming, sweetheart. It's more than enough to replace the boat and get set up again, once this blows over. Nicky's got no proof, and he can't go to the police. It'll all die down and we'll go on as before, you'll see."

"I wish I could share your optimism. You told me Nicky Luchesse has certain connections, isn't that right?" Ella stood, and called out to the children. "Time to get out of the pool, you guys." She turned to Jevaun. "I only hope they're not the type of connections who leave young children without a father."

An involuntary shiver went down Jevaun's spine as he watched Ella shoo the children inside. His family was his life. He paused, before lifting his phone and pressing the last called button.

"Bob, it's Jevaun," he said, when the call was answered seconds later. "Were you looking for me?"

"The Skipper is," Bob said. "The candy's been checked over, and it's ready for pickup. He wants a word with you about the last lot. To make sure it doesn't happen again, if you catch my drift."

Jevaun checked his watch. "Sure. The replacement boat I've arranged to borrow is docked in George Town. I'll be with you as soon as I can. Tell Nicky I'd be happy to speak to him to reassure him nothing will go wrong this time. He can count on me."

"I hope so." Bob didn't sound convinced.

Jevaun regretted his slipup with Bob a few months earlier. When he'd hinted there could be something in it for Bob if he ever wanted to 'come in' with Jevaun on a deal, Bob had made his loyalty to Nicky very clear.

"I'm not sure what you mean, man," Bob had said with a tip of his cap. "And I've no reason to know about any deals that don't include the Skipper.

With Bob on his side, Jevaun might have had an easier time convincing Nicky the shipment had been stolen and the boat destroyed while the crew had gotten drunk in a bar in Cuba. As it was, Bob was far too loyal to Nicky for Jevaun to risk trying to bribe him in a last-ditch attempt to have him be his backup.

Jevaun made a snap decision. "See you soon, Bob."

There was nothing else he could do. To make his problem go away, he would have to make Nicky go away. That partner of Nicky's in Chicago was unlikely to cause any trouble, especially if Jevaun told him it was Nicky who had screwed them both over and stolen the shipment. And if push came to shove, he could take care of Benny too.

*Yes, that should do the trick. And when the money comes through I can put all this behind me and get back to business as usual. We all make mistakes. Nicky's mistake was doubting me in the first place.*

# CHAPTER TEN

DeeDee and Cassie had moved to a swinging seat in the garden to wait for the men to return.

"Here's Jake now," DeeDee said, hopeful of some reprieve from the ominous churning in her stomach.

Jake strode towards them with a solemn expression. When he got closer, he caught DeeDee's eye and shook his head, telling her all she needed to know before he'd so much as uttered a word.

"Nicky's dead," he said, when he came to a stop beside the seat. He stuffed his hands in his pants pockets. "He was shot. There's nothing we could do. We found him too late. Al spotted the body lying on the jetty from one of the upstairs windows. He's just called 911. The Royal Cayman Islands Police Service are on the way."

DeeDee was glad she was sitting down, because her legs had turned to jelly. She turned to Cassie, who appeared more composed than she was, but only by the slimmest of margins.

"Poor Nicky," DeeDee mumbled, although she'd never met him.

"I'll make coffee," Cassie said, ever practical. She eased herself to her feet. "And see if we can make use of the food in the kitchen. I expect it's going to be a long night. If I know Al, he's going to want to get to the bottom of this."

"You'd be right, Cassie." Jake frowned. "Al's not taking it well at all. He said he'll be along in a little while. He doesn't want to leave Nicky by himself, so he's waiting with the body until the first responders get here."

"That's typical of Al," Cassie said, her voice soft. Her words echoed what DeeDee was thinking. "He wouldn't like Nicky to be alone. Al's made me promise if he dies before me, I'll stay with him until he's cremated. He doesn't want to be buried you see, in case there's been a mistake and he gets buried alive."

Despite herself, DeeDee smiled. The thought of Al trying to escape from his own coffin just about summed him up. When Al's time came, there was no way he was going quietly, of that she was certain. She could hear the sound of sirens approaching. "I'll help you in the kitchen, Cassie."

"I guess I'd better go open the gates," Jake said. "It sounds like the police have arrived."

*****

Later that night, Cassie, DeeDee, and Jake sat in silence at the dining room table in Nicky's house, waiting for Al to speak. Al was pacing back and forth in the kitchen, his hands balled into fists. Nicky's body had been loaded onto a gurney and then taken away in an ambulance. The police had left after taking statements from all four of them.

"We gotta' find out who killed Nicky," Al said at last. DeeDee could see the veins pulsing in his temples. "This is personal. The Detective Superintendent said he'd be in touch if they come up with anythin', but I ain't holdin' my breath. Somethin' tells me, based on the kinda' business Nicky was involved in, finding his murderer might not be the local police force's highest priority. Plus, they're a small team."

"Count me in," Jake said.

"Me too," Cassie chimed in.

All eyes turned to DeeDee. "Me three."

A trace of a smile crossed Al's lips, and he pulled out a chair and sat down beside Cassie. She reached out and squeezed his hand.

"Thanks," Al said, "I appreciate it. Me an' Nicky go way back. Once family, always family, is how it works in the Mafia. I know he woulda' done the same for me." He swallowed, his eyes wet.

Faced with his obvious distress, DeeDee felt herself choking up for the big man sitting opposite her who wore his heart on his sleeve. His tough guy persona was a front for what those people close to him knew. Al De Duco would lay himself down in front of any enemy to help anyone he cared about and would consider it a not only matter of honor, but a privilege, to do so. Once Al was on your side he never wavered. No questions asked.

"Nicky's housekeeper, Sharisha, is on her way over," Al said, drumming his fingers on the table. "I called her as soon as the police left to let her know they'd be contactin' her and the other members of Nicky's staff. I wanted Sharisha to hear the news from someone she knew. She was very upset, said she'd be right here."

"Who else did Nicky employ?" Jake asked.

Al thought for a moment. "There's a pool boy and a gardener, who both come by once a week. Sharisha is here every day. I think her husband might help around the place with some handywork whenever Nicky needed household repairs or manual labor. I'm not sure if her husband was here today, but we'll soon find out."

When Sharisha arrived, DeeDee made more coffee. A tiny black woman, Sharisha sobbed for a long time before Al could get any information from her. "My Mr. Nicky," was all she could say, wailing into a handful of wet tissue paper. Al pulled a clean handkerchief from his pocket and handed it to her. "Thank you, Mr. Al," she said, pressing the cool linen against her face and dabbing her eyes. When she was done, she offered it back to Al.

"That's okay, you keep it, Sharisha," he said gently. "I know this is distressing for ya', but when's the last time ya' saw Nicky? Were ya' here today?"

Sharisha nodded. "Yes, sir. Mr. Nicky asked me to get everything ready for you and Ms. Cassie and your friends who were coming to dinner." She gave DeeDee and Jake a shy smile. "I saw him this morning, and he told me he would be going out to do some work with Bob on one of the boats. He said for me to go home whenever I was done. When I left, Mr. Nicky wasn't back."

Al pushed his cell phone across the table to Jake. "Jake, take this and look up the number for Bob Ennis. He's in charge of Nicky's boats and crew, and I know him pretty well. Call him and explain who ya' are and tell him we're gonna' need names and phone numbers for the rest of the crew. Ask him the usual questions. Ya' know the drill. What time he left Nicky, and if there was anythin' else goin' on we need to know about. I jes' have a few more things to run through with Sharisha, and I'll be right with ya'."

"Sure thing, Al. Excuse me, folks," Jake said, getting up from the table. "I won't be long."

DeeDee could hear him speaking on the phone in the hallway, until he went into the great room and closed the door.

Al turned his attention back to Sharisha. "Was there anyone else at the house today? Anyone who worked for Nicky, or was he expectin' any company?"

She shook her head. "No sir, not that I know of. Lee, the pool boy, usually comes on Saturdays, but Nicky gave him the day off for the same reason he told me to go home early…" Her voice trailed off to a whisper.

"Why was that?" DeeDee said, coaxing her to continue.

"Today's a Rastafarian holy day. November 2 is the commemoration of the Crowning of Emperor Haile Selassie I. He was an Ethiopian king." Sharisha sniffed. "And now, this date will always be for me to remember Mr. Nicky as well." She bowed her head.

"Nicky had a girlfriend, Sharisha," Al said carefully. "Devan Parker, is that right?"

Sharisha looked up, startled, like a deer caught in headlights.

Al's eyes narrowed. "What is it, Sharisha? Was Devan here today, visiting Nicky?"

"Mr. Al, I don't know. I told you, I saw nothing. Mr. Nicky's lady friends are none of my business."

"Do you mean lady friend...or friends?" Al leaned in closer to Sharisha. "Please, Sharisha, this is important. Was Nicky seein' more than one woman?" He glanced at Cassie and DeeDee. "Wouldn't surprise me."

Sharisha sat in silence, staring at the table.

Al tried again. "I know Nicky has cameras, so I'll be goin' through all the footage. I can go back as far as it takes until I find somethin'. But it would be a lot quicker if you would tell us now Sharisha, who Nicky was seein', in case they know anythin' about his death. Ya' want to help us find whoever did this, right?"

She nodded.

"And the police will want to know too. You'd be better off tellin' ol' Mr. Al, huh?"

Sharisha hesitated. When she did speak up her voice was quiet but clear. "Lady Gwendolyn Blackwood was Mr. Nicky's other lady friend, sir."

Al let out a low whistle. "Well, Nicky Luchesse was an' ol' devil, I'll give him that." He patted Sharisha's hand. "Thanks fer all your help, sweetheart. If ya' need anythin' come and see me, got it? How did ya' get here, do ya' need a ride home?"

"My husband is waiting outside, Mr. Al. He will take me home."

Al stood and helped Sharisha up, seeing her to the door. When he returned, he was accompanied by Jake.

"Bob left around 5:00 pm," Jake said, checking his notes. "Nicky and Bob had been looking after some business on one of Nicky's boats moored off the jetty when Nicky returned to the house. Bob was waiting for a guy called Jevaun Henriques to show up. Do you know him?"

Al nodded. "Yeah. Go on."

"Well, Bob got a call from home and had to leave before Jevaun arrived. Bob has an old speedboat he uses to get from here to his village a few miles down the coast. He phoned Nicky on his cell to let him know, but there was no reply. He left a voice message and headed off." Jake looked up. "We can easily check that with the call history on Nicky's phone, or the phone company can verify it if necessary."

"Did Bob say why Jevaun was coming over?" DeeDee asked him.

"Nope, he wouldn't say," Jake replied.

Al spoke up. "I think I know, but I'll speak to Bob about it myself. The police will want to talk to him as well, which makes things slightly more complicated. I'll have to think that one over." He rubbed his chin, while DeeDee and Cassie filled Jake in on what Sharisha had told them about Nicky having two girlfriends.

"Let's start with Lady Gwendolyn Blackwood," Al said, when

they'd made a list of the names they had so far. "I don't know the woman, so I think Jake should cover her. With a title like that, she won't be hard to track down. I'd be better off speakin' to Bob Ennis first thing. I know some of the background with Jevaun Henriques, so Bob can fill me in on the latest."

DeeDee peered at the list. "Who's next, Devan Parker?"

"We'll have to figure out where to find her," Al said. "DeeDee, Cassie, how about you two start lookin' through the security camera footage tomorrow and see if we can get a description of her and a car license plate? The film might provide some other clues as well."

"Sure," DeeDee said, glancing at Cassie for confirmation. Cassie nodded. "We can do that."

Al wrote another name on the list. "Ima gonn'a have to speak with Nicky's business partner in Chicago, Benny Amato, and tell him what's happened, if he don't already know. In fact, I think Ima gonna' do that tonight."

"Why's Benny on the list, Al, if they were business partners? And how could Benny know Nicky's dead?" It was Cassie's turn to look confused.

Al chuckled. "Ever hear the phrase 'Keep your friends close, and your enemies closer?' It applies to the Mafioso more than most." He looked around the table. "Let's call it a night folks, cuz' tomorrow, we ain't goin' fishin', we're goin' on a murder hunt."

# CHAPTER ELEVEN

The Blackwood residence wasn't that hard to find. Teddy had sat at the kitchen island preparing a map of the route in painstaking detail. The finished result was a page containing lots of squiggly lines, annotated with undecipherable writing. Teddy talked Jake through the directions before he set off.

"This is the best way to get there," Teddy had said, tracing his finger along the handmade map. "See? You can take this short cut to get there quicker." He'd given Jake a beaming smile, handing over his artwork.

"How will I know which house it is?" Jake had asked him, confused. There were so many arrows on the page, it looked more like a meteorological report rather than a document explaining how to get somewhere that Teddy had assured him was only a few miles away.

"You'll know when you see it," Teddy said with a wise nod. "Mr. Jake not stupid."

The morning after Nicky's body had been discovered on the jetty, Jake set off in Al's Lamborghini roadster, hoping Teddy was right. If he couldn't follow the map, he figured he could always stop and ask for directions. The top was down, and the wind blew Jake's hair back as he sped along the island roads, slowing for pedestrians in vibrant

George Town, and once for a chicken meandering across the street in a village near Bodden Bay.

Little children waved at him, and he honked the horn and waved back. The coastal route was stunning, a rainbow of colorful houses on one side of the road, and the light aqua blue of the shallow reef waters on the other. Swimmers and snorkelers bobbed in the water near the shore. Further out in the water, jet skis zipped across the sea.

Jake squinted at Teddy's map. All the arrows were pointing in the direction of Pease Bay on the south side of the island. The pale waters of the shallow reef on the western shores had given way to crystal blue and crashing waves. Jake cruised past residential developments that looked like they belonged to permanent residents, rather than the glitzy holiday rentals that were in abundance in the tourist area of Seven Mile Beach.

When he saw the imposing manor house from a distance, he smiled. Teddy was right. That had to be it. It looked like an English stately home right out of an historical movie. He turned in through the open front gates and followed a winding driveway leading to a pillared entrance with steps up to a grand door with a golden lion's head attached to it for a door knocker.

Like the grounds, which were impressive but not manicured, Jake noticed the house was more tired-looking up close than upon first impressions from afar. Two cars were parked out front, a Bentley and a Jaguar, both several years old.

The lion's head made a resounding thump when Jake knocked it twice against the door, whose paint was cracked and starting to peel away in places. He heard footsteps coming towards the door and when it creaked open he was greeted by a middle-aged maid dressed in traditional black and white attire.

"Good afternoon," the maid said in a formal tone. "Welcome to the Blackwood residence. May I help you?"

"I'm here to see Lady Blackwood," Jake said, matching her tone.

The maid stared at him with no trace of a smile. "Is she expecting you? Sir Alec and Lady Gwendolyn never receive company on Sundays."

"No, we haven't met." He fished a business card from his pocket and handed it to her. "Could you please tell her it's Jake Rogers, a private investigator from the United States? It's concerning Nicky Luchesse."

The maid checked the card before nodding. "Very well, sir. Please wait here." She left the door open as she scurried down a hall.

From his vantage point on the doorstep, Jake could see that the interior of the house was like a time warp. Family portraits hung on the wood-paneled walls and threadbare rugs lined the floors. From what he could tell, the structure was sound, but it looked like the maintenance and decor had been neglected for a long time. It was probably nothing a large six-figure sum couldn't put right.

Several minutes later, the maid returned. "Please, follow me, Mr. Rogers. Lady Gwendolyn will be with you shortly." She led him down the hallway into a formal sitting room, with winged chairs and a piano in the corner. "Would you like some tea?"

The maid's cold manner led Jake to believe she very much did not want to make him tea, and he shook his head. "No, thanks. I'm good."

"Very well." She nodded and left the room, clicking the door shut.

Jake didn't sit, instead he walked around the room, noting the ornaments and silver candelabras on the mantel, and the ancient coal scuttle by the hearth. Framed photographs adorned every available surface, depicting images from another century. No one in the photos was smiling. The overwhelming feeling Jake got was of coldness. Despite its fading grandeur, the house was a showcase, not a home.

Raised voices in the hallway caused him to step closer to the door.

A woman was speaking. "Go away, Alec, I'll deal with this."

"Why is some Yank showing up here asking questions about Nicky Luchesse, and what does it have to do with you? That's what I'd like to know."

"Alec, please." The woman sounded upset. "It's probably nothing. Just leave it to me."

"Good riddance to Luchesse, that's all I can say. Never met the chap, but the island doesn't need his sort."

"What's that supposed to mean? If you've never met him, what are you so antsy about?"

"Gwendolyn, I swear I'll—"

Jake swung the door open. "Everything all right out here?"

Lady Gwendolyn turned to Jake with a look of relief. She stepped forward and extended her hand. "Hello, Mr. Rogers, I'm Gwendolyn Blackwood. This is my husband, Alec."

Jake shook Gwendolyn's hand and turned to her husband.

"It's Sir Alec, to you," the short man said, giving Jake a perfunctory handshake. "And we're busy, so please don't take up much of my wife's time." He glared at Jake and turned on his heel, stomping off. Jake thought the term Little Man Syndrome had probably been invented for people like Sir Alec.

Jake followed Lady Gwendolyn into the parlor, or whatever function the little sitting room was supposed to serve. When he sat down in one of the winged chairs as motioned by the lady of the house, he realized it wasn't anywhere near as comfortable as it looked. The seat was as hard as a rock.

"As you probably heard, Mr. Rogers, I have no idea why you are here." Gwendolyn twisted her hands in her lap. "My husband and I don't know Mr. Luchesse. We heard on the local news this morning he has departed this life for his final resting place. Apart from despairing at the violent criminals who live in our community, I have nothing to add on the matter."

"I see." Jake watched her in silence, noting her sense of discomfort under his gaze. Not catching his eye, she chewed on her lower lip. Attractive in an English rose sort of way, her pale cheeks were flushed, and her hair unkempt. The smudged dark eye liner around her eyes indicated she was either going for a rock star makeup look, which he doubted, or that she'd been crying. "I thought it was your husband who said he'd never met Nicky Luchesse, Lady Gwendolyn. You, on the other hand, knew him rather well, didn't you?"

Gwendolyn met his gaze with fire in her eyes. "How dare you," she hissed. "I have no idea what you mean."

Jake lowered his voice. "There is security camera footage, Lady Gwendolyn, that shows you were a regular visitor to Nicky's home near Seven Mile Beach. Your car, the same Jaguar that's parked out front, was parked at Nicky's residence numerous times during the past couple of months. Nicky was murdered yesterday evening at some time between 5:00 p.m. and 8:00 p.m. Is there anything you'd like to tell me before I share the video evidence with the police?"

Gwendolyn's face crumpled. Her voice was a whisper. "I may have been at Nicky's place once or twice, but I wasn't there yesterday, so you couldn't have seen my car there. I was attending a charity function, and in any case, my husband has been using my car for the last few days since his has been acting up."

Jake wasn't about to tell Lady Gwendolyn the security cameras at Nicky's home had been off the previous day, much to his and Al's dismay when they checked the most recent recordings. They'd only had time that morning to look at the footage going back a few weeks, but Jake had taken a gamble that since Lady Gwendolyn had visited Nicky several times during that period, it was probably a regular pattern.

Instead, he said, "Oh, so it's Nicky now? Maybe you should start at the beginning, Lady Gwendolyn."

"You mustn't tell my husband," Gwendolyn pleaded. "You already saw and heard how annoyed he was. Please, at least let me tell him myself."

Jake pulled out a notebook. "I'll leave that to your discretion, Lady Gwendolyn. Please, go ahead whenever you're ready. And don't omit anything or embellish the truth."

Gwendolyn's story came tumbling out along with her tears. She had met Nicky several years earlier at one of her charity events when he'd bid a large amount for one of the auction items. "He pursued me like no one has ever done before, Mr. Rogers," Gwendolyn explained. "He wouldn't take no for an answer. He wore me down until I couldn't resist his charms any longer. He was funny, and considerate, and…"

"Very rich?"

Gwendolyn scowled. "Yes, that as well. But I wasn't just with him for his money, although he was very generous, and the gifts were nice. I wanted more, but Nicky wasn't willing to settle down. He made that clear from the start, so I broke up with him. For a long time, I avoided events where I knew he might be in attendance. There were various charitable causes that were close to his heart, and I made sure I was unavailable to serve on any of those committees."

"Go on, please." Jake continued taking notes.

"I bumped into him again several months ago, and we talked. I'd forgotten how he made me feel…he was hard to resist."

"Clearly." Jake raised an eyebrow. "So, you reconciled?"

She nodded. "This time, it was more intense than before. I really thought he might change his mind about settling down. I thought we might even start a family together…but it seems that I was wrong."

"How so, Lady Gwendolyn?"

"I found out Nicky was seeing someone else," she said. "In fact, it was my friend Marion Bartlett who told me about it earlier this week. We're on several fundraising committees together. She attended the charity function I was at yesterday. It was a cocktails event at the Kimpton Seafire Resort."

"And Ms. Bartlett can vouch for your whereabouts between 5:00 p.m. and 8:00 p.m. yesterday evening?"

"That's correct, along with several hundred others, I imagine. It was very well attended. You'd have to check with Marla, our maid, to find out what time I returned by taxi, but I think it was around 9:00 p.m." She frowned. "Quite a lot of gin was involved, so I don't exactly remember. I'm not quite myself today, and what with the news about Nicky…" Her voice trailed off.

Jake tapped his pen on the notebook. "Could your husband vouch for what time you returned home, Lady Gwendolyn?"

She shrugged. "No, he wasn't here. He plays golf every Saturday afternoon and usually has a few drinks at the nineteenth hole afterwards."

"What time did your husband return home?"

Gwendolyn stood up, raising a hand to her forehead. "Mr. Rogers, you'll have to ask Alec that. I'm not my husband's keeper. Now if that's all, I'm not feeling very well. Marla will see you to the door."

Jake was left staring with a bemused smile at the open doorway as Lady Gwendolyn flounced out of the room.

# CHAPTER TWELVE

Al stalked up behind the bald-headed man sitting at the bar and gave him a hearty slap on the shoulder. "Yo, Benny."

The man turned his head around and gave him a twisted smile. "Hey, De Duco. Fancy seeing you here."

Al cocked his head towards several empty tables by the windows. They were in the Grand Cayman Marriott Beach Resort, where Benny was staying. "Let's go over there. It's quiet in here this time of day, but I wanna' make sure we're not overheard."

Benny stood up and reaching in his pocket, pushed a handful of bills across the counter. "Two more beers please," he said to the bartender. "We'll be over by the windows."

Al and Benny made their way to an open area next to the windows that was furnished with wicker armchairs lined with thick pillows, and carved wooden tree trunks as tables. Double-story windows looked out onto the garden, which was empty apart from a hotel worker sweeping the pathway. Al waited until the bartender had left after delivering their beers before he began to speak.

Meeting in public wasn't an ideal location for Al. He would have invited Benny to his place, but with Jake gone to see Lady Gwendolyn, he didn't want to endanger Cassie or DeeDee in case there was any trouble. He didn't think Benny would pull a gun on him in a hotel bar, but with Benny Amato there were no guarantees. He was known in Mafia circles as a hothead with a reputation for acting first and thinking later.

"Shame about Nicky," Benny said, lifting his beer bottle. "I'll miss him."

"You an' me both." Al watched Benny take a gulp of his beer. "I was surprised when I called ya' last night, Benny, and ya' said you were in town. I thought ya'd be in Chicago. You don't come over here much, do ya'?"

Benny shrugged. "Sometimes I do, sometimes I don't."

Al leaned closer. "I'll get straight to the point, Benny. Do ya' know who killed Nicky?"

Benny laughed. "Are you asking if I killed him? No, Al, I didn't. He was my long-time business partner. Why would I do something stupid like that?" He swirled his beer around in its bottle, holding Al's gaze.

"Seems strange you're in town at the same time as Nicky got murdered, that's all."

"Really? I could say the same for you."

Al gave Benny an exaggerated eye roll. "I found him, Benny. If I'd whacked him, I wouldn't be hangin' around."

"Do you think I would either? Come on, buddy. You know me better than that. I'm not stupid. I'd be on and off the island before anyone knew I was even here. It would be easy for me to charter a boat that no one saw coming or going. I know all the out-of-the-way coves, remember? But no, I arrived on the afternoon flight from Miami, and I'm sticking around for several days. Might as well enjoy myself while I'm here."

Benny leaned back in his seat and lifted one foot across his other thigh, resting his elbow on the raised leg.

Al knew Benny's body language was well thought out. No casual relaxing for him. Infamous in Chicago for having passed a lie detector test when the Feds called him up as a witness in a high-profile Mafia money-laundering investigation, Benny had shot up the family ranks as a result.

"So why are ya' here, Benny, if not to murder your business partner? Nicky told me ya' don't come over very often. I thought he dealt with things on this side."

Benny thought for a few moments. "That's true, but we've been having a few logistical problems, unreliable transportation, cargo going missing, that sort of thing. I needed to see Nicky in person to try and get to the bottom of it. Stem the bleeding, call it what you like. Too much money at stake not to."

"I hear ya', Benny, I hear ya'. Nicky mentioned it a coupla' times, but not the details. So, what's been going on?"

Benny's eyes darted around the area where they were sitting to make sure no one was within earshot. "We're down a couple of mill ever since a boat went missing. The guy who does the candy run says the boat was stolen during the layover in Cuba. The crew was in a bar while the boat was getting refuelled. Next thing you know, the crew got drunk and when they came back the following morning the boat was gone. A few days later, bits of the hull washed up near Havana, and it looks like the boat's been torched. Or, at least that's how Nicky told it."

"Didn'tcha believe him?"

"I don't know what to believe, Al." Benny let out a heavy sigh.

Al thought he saw a flicker of something cloud his expression. *Worry? Regret? Guilt?* he wondered.

In an instant, the look was gone, and Benny continued. "Here's the thing. The boat should never have been left unattended. I know that, Nicky knows that, the candy man knows that. Heck, you know that. But just suppose for a minute, that the boat really was stolen and torched. Do you honestly think the candy went up with it? Because I sure don't."

"Good point. So, who do you think took the candy?"

"That's the two-million-dollar question, my friend. Way I see it, there's three possibilities. One, it was looted by a third party. Two, it was a set-up orchestrated by the candy man. Three, Nicky and the candy man were complicit. Whatever the answer, Benny's piece of the pie has disappeared."

"Hmm." Al was loath to admit it, but Benny had a point. "And you wanna' know who stole your pie, right?"

"Right."

It was Al's turn to sigh. "I'm certain Nicky didn't rip ya' off, Benny, but I can kinda' understand why you might think that. You gotta' cover all the bases. If I was in your shoes, I'd probably reach the same conclusion."

A worrying thought occurred to him. *What if I didn't know the real Nicky? The two women he was keepin' was news to me.* He pushed it out of his mind.

"Want another beer, Al?" Benny looked around to catch the bartender's attention. "I'm sitting here on empty."

Al shook his head. He hadn't touched his. "I'm good, thanks. Benny. Did Nicky ever tell ya' about the two women he was seein'?"

Benny chuckled. "Not the details, thankfully, but yes, I knew about them. I don't think Nicky was particularly proud of the situation, which is why he didn't broadcast it, along with the fact that one of the women is married."

Al's tension eased. That explanation made sense. He was silent while the waiter served Benny his beer. Aware of a party of four approaching where they were sitting, he caught Benny's eye.

Benny nodded and placed a bundle of cash on the waiter's tray. "We don't want to be disturbed in here. Can you arrange that, please, along with a round of drinks for the party who are on their way over, but are about to be disappointed?"

"Of course, gentlemen." The waiter expertly diverted the other guests to another part of the lounge, leaving the two men from Chicago alone once more.

Al nursed his beer. "The candy man, is it the same guy you've been usin' for a while? Guy that goes by the name of Jevaun Henriques?"

Benny nodded. "He's the one. Lives in a commune with his own private harem and a crowd of kids he's fathered with the various women he's collected over the years."

"Ima gonna speak to Bob tomorrow and see what he thinks," Al said. "I wasn't able to reach him this mornin'. Heard it was some kind of religious festival yesterday, so maybe that's the reason his phone's still off."

"If you speak to Bob before I do, tell him not to tip off the candy man I'm looking for him." Benny tapped the end of his unlit cigar several times on the table to tamp it down. "I'd rather surprise him myself. I'll leave you to do the Columbo thing and hunt down Nicky's murderer, while I try and find out what happened to the candy."

"Do ya' even care about Nicky?" Al slammed his beer bottle on the table. "Ya' worked with him for what, thirty years? And all you're worried about is the candy? Geez, Benny. I thought more of ya' than that. Oh, and ya' can't smoke in here."

Benny stood up. "I wasn't about to. I'm going outside."

"Hey, Benny." Al's voice was far louder than it should have been for someone not wanting to attract attention. As it was, several people from tables in the main bar area turned and looked in their direction.

"Settle down, big guy." Benny's tone was menacing. His arm was wrapped around to the side of his waistband, hovering above the spot where Al knew a weapon was concealed.

Al reached inside the bottom of his trouser leg, ready to pull his piece if Benny reached for his. He imagined the headlines if either of them so much as twitched. *Shoot out at the Grand Cayman Marriott Beach Resort.* That wouldn't get them anywhere. Al wasn't afraid of dying, but he didn't want Cassie to be a widow again.

"Ya' said you flew in yesterday on the afternoon flight from Miami. Unless ya' can tell me where ya' were between 5:00 p.m. which is when Bob left Nicky's, and 8:00 p.m. when I arrived with my friends, that puts ya' center stage in the murder investigation. Whaddya' say to that, Benny?"

"I'd say you should speak to the Airport Police. I was detained at Immigration for six hours. I called Nicky when the flight landed, then I got hauled over inside the terminal. They gave me a full-body search, swabs, the works." Benny's face was deadpan, his eyes unblinking. "Not a pleasant experience. But it's a good alibi, you have to admit."

"Oh, I'll speak to 'em, alright." Al watched as Benny stepped backwards towards the door to the garden, their eyes never leaving each other the whole time. Al's hand did not waver until Benny pushed the door behind him and stepped outside. "I'll be seein' ya, Benny."

"Sure thing, Al. You take care." Benny chuckled and lit his cigar.

# CHAPTER THIRTEEN

The next morning, just after they'd finished breakfast, Al said, "Cassie, the driver's coming to pick you and DeeDee up at 11:00 a.m. to take you to George Town. Ima gonna' stop by the police station before I meet Bob Ennis. I wanna' know if Benny's alibi checks out. Then Ima hopin' Bob can give me the skinny on whatever he thinks Jevaun's been up to. Have a nice day exploring the shops in George Town, you two." He lifted his phone from the table and stuffed it in his pocket.

DeeDee looked over from where she was stacking the breakfast dishes in the dishwasher. "Al, are you sure Cassie and I can't help you and Jake with anything today? We can go shopping another time."

Al shook his head. "Nope, you should take a break. Y'all spent yesterday lookin' through Nicky's security camera tapes. Jake can cover that while I'm gone. I know ya' want to pick up a few things, and we can all catch up later and see what we've got. How does that sound?"

"Alright, if you insist." DeeDee smiled at Cassie, who had told her before their visit there was no sales tax in the Caymans, so there were plenty of good buys to be had. DeeDee knew Cassie was determined to have a piece of jewelry made with the semi-precious stone, caymanite.

DeeDee had read about the Cayman Sea Salt Company, the only salt producer on the island, who made gourmet salt by evaporating seawater in the sun to produce salt crystals. She was planning on buying some.

"Jake, ya' wanna' ride to Nicky's place?" Al asked him. "I'll buzz ya' in."

"Sure." Jake kissed DeeDee lightly and said, "See you later. Have fun, and don't spend your kids' inheritance."

"Too late," DeeDee replied with a grin. "It's already long gone."

The town car the two women had ordered pulled up in front of the house several minutes before 11:00 a.m., Teddy having opened the gates earlier.

The driver opened the door, and DeeDee and Cassie slipped into the comfy leather seats in the back, which was spacious enough to have accommodated Red and Holt as well. Both dogs were standing in the driveway, peering inside the car, hoping for a ride.

"Not today, you two," Cassie said, shooing them away before the door closed.

DeeDee could see Teddy commanding the dogs to retreat to the house.

The driver viewed them through the rearview mirror. "Where to, ladies?"

"Downtown George Town, please," Cassie said. "We're going shopping. Where would you recommend?"

By the time the car pulled up to the bustling Craft Market located on the waterfront, DeeDee had typed the driver's shopping tips into her phone—Kirk Freeport for high end brands, Artifacts for unique gifts, Arabus for elegant clothing, and Rocky's Diamond Gallery for precious jewelry.

"I can fit four sets of golf clubs in the trunk, so there'll be plenty of room for all your shopping treasures," he assured them with a laugh as they climbed out.

"Oh, I don't think we'll be going crazy," Cassie said with a smile. "My husband's the extravagant one, not me."

DeeDee had always admired how restrained Cassie was with her spending. Considering her friend's wealth, she wasn't flashy. Ignoring Al's protestations, on Bainbridge Island Cassie still drove a beat-up old station wagon she'd owned for years. That, despite the fact her first husband had owned an immensely successful Mercedes Benz dealership before he was murdered, was something even DeeDee found hard to comprehend.

Armed with the driver's card and instructions to call him whenever they were ready for him to come and pick them up, DeeDee and Cassie set off to explore George Town.

Cassie's only time on the island had been limited to a couple of brief trips with Al. "He has the patience of a flea when it comes to shopping," she said as they wandered around the market. "As soon as we arrive in one store he's ready to jump to the next. He has no concept of browsing, or window shopping just for the sake of it. I'm glad you're here, DeeDee. Shopping with girlfriends is much more fun."

"So true," DeeDee said as she picked up a shell bracelet she thought her daughter, Tink, would like. "I think it's a man thing. Jake's not quite that bad, but he definitely doesn't get it. He thinks there's no reason to go shopping unless you need something, in which case he zones in on that one thing, and then he's done. Where's the fun in that?"

They both agreed there was none.

By the time they arrived at Lobster Pot a couple of hours later for lunch, they had not only had a lot of fun, they had quite a few shopping bags between them. They were seated by the hostess at an outside table with a panoramic view of the waterfront.

"Let me see the caymanite again," DeeDee said, after they'd ordered a bottle of wine which they intended to share. She pointed to the bag from a store in Kennedy Gallery, where Cassie had bought an exquisite chunk of the natural stone that was found within the cliffs of Grand Cayman.

Cassie opened the bag and pulled out a box, inside of which the semi-precious stone was nestled in tissue paper. Unwrapping it, she handed it to DeeDee, who turned it over in her hand. Natural and unpolished, alternate shades of beige were tinged with a metallic hue. Its size was big enough to be carved into a substantial and striking pendant, and all for a price that while not cheap, was not out of most tourist's range. The fact that the stone was only available locally in the Cayman Islands added to its desirability. "It's gorgeous," DeeDee said, handing it back. "I can't wait to see the finished necklace you're going to have made with it."

A waitress approached the table.

"We haven't looked at the menu, but I don't think we need to," DeeDee said. "We'll have the lobster pot, please."

Cassie nodded in agreement. "And a side salad and bread. Thank you."

"I think I'd like to go back and have another look in Artifacts," DeeDee said while they waited for the food. "It was like a treasure trove in there." Crammed with antique jewelery, maps, prints, china, and shipwreck treasures, it struck her as the perfect place to buy a unique gift. "I'd like to pick up something for Roz."

"Sure, we can do that. How are the twins, by the way?" Cassie asked her.

"Adorable," DeeDee said, pulling out her phone to show Cassie the latest photos. Roz, her sister, had given birth to baby Vinny and baby Em several months earlier. "I think Roz is exhausted, but she's loving every minute of being a mom. And they're pretty good babies, especially Vinny."

"Al will probably take the credit for that, if you'll let him," Cassie said as she scrolled through the photos of the twins and showed them to DeeDee. "He takes his godfather duties very seriously. Did I tell you I heard him singing to them on Facetime? It was Row, Row, Row Your Boat. He even had Red barking along."

DeeDee leaned back while the food was served. She smiled up at the waitress. "Thank you." To Cassie, she said with a laugh, "Roz told me. She has it recorded, in case we ever need to embarrass him."

"Embarass Al?" Cassie took the lid off the pot and began to dissect the lobster. She shook her head. "I'm not sure that's possible."

The women proceeded to enjoy a leisurely lunch. The chilled bottle of chardonnay was the perfect pairing for the freshly caught lobster drenched in melted butter. They chatted about family, work, travel, and food, Cassie sharing some of the highs and lows of her recent Food Spy column reviews. When Cassie stopped mid-sentence and stared in stunned silence at something which had caught her attention behind DeeDee, DeeDee's first reaction was to turn around.

"Don't look now," Cassie said, wide-eyed. She covered the side of her mouth with her hand. "I think I've just seen Devan Parker."

It took DeeDee a moment to register who Cassie meant. She kept her voice down. "Really? Are you sure?"

Cassie nodded. "Pretty sure, but I need you to check and make sure I'm not going crazy. Can you walk past where she's sitting and see if it's definitely her? She's at one o'clock from where I'm sitting."

"Sure." DeeDee put her napkin down and reached for her purse, turning as she rose and walked towards the Ladies Room, while scanning to her right as she did so. She and Cassie had seen Devan on the camera footage they'd been looking through the previous day. Having been struck then by the young woman's beauty and facing her now in real life as she was engaged in close conversation with a male companion, DeeDee noted she looked even more beautiful and vibrant in the flesh. Devan's glowing limbs seemed to go on forever, her exquisite face seemingly sculpted atop a swanlike neck. DeeDee had no doubt that Cassie was right.

Settling the check while she was gone, she texted Cassie from the Ladies Room to confirm that she agreed it was Devan. DeeDee returned to the table just as Devan and her companion were leaving, Cassie got to her feet, and the two women followed the couple out onto the street, being careful to remain several paces behind Devan and her friend.

It wasn't long before the pair stopped outside a glass office building in the business district, where the man kissed Devan on the lips before placing a hand on the small of her back as they walked inside. The sign on the building read, 'Goldstone Bank.'

Waiting for a few moments to make sure the woman didn't come out again, DeeDee and Cassie approached the doorman.

"Excuse me," DeeDee said with a smile. "I thought that was a friend of mine who just went in. Do you know if that was Devan Parker?"

"That's correct, ma'am. She works here."

DeeDee made a face. "I can't believe I just missed her. What time does the bank close? I'll try and catch her after work."

"4:00 p.m., ma'am."

"Thanks so much. I'll come back later."

Stepping away, DeeDee looked at Cassie. "Are you thinking what I'm thinking?"

"You tell me. I was going to suggest calling the driver and arranging for him to meet us here at 4:00 p.m. We can follow Devan home and speak to her in private." Cassie raised an eyebrow. "Was it something along those lines?"

"Yep." DeeDee checked her watch. "I guess we still have time to go back to Artifacts. As well as picking up something for Roz, I saw an old map there that I thought Jake might like. He was admiring the ones in Nicky's hallway, so I guess he must have an interest in old maps."

"Hmm." Cassie tucked a wisp of hair behind her ear. She was growing out her pixie cut, and several strands had gone rogue around her hairline. "I'm not sure if Al got around to explaining to Jake his newfound interest in old maps of this area."

DeeDee gave her a quizzical look. "Come to think of it, you're right. Anything you want to share with me?"

"Oh no, I'll leave that to Al," Cassie said. "I wouldn't want to steal his thunder. In any case, something tells me with Nicky's death, it's off the agenda for now. But knowing Al, it will come up again."

"I'm intrigued," DeeDee said as she picked up her shopping bags. "Come on, let's go. We've got more pressing priorities to attend to."

# CHAPTER FOURTEEN

When DeeDee and Cassie returned, they stashed their shopping purchases upstairs before going outside, where they found Jake and Al sitting at a table next to the pool and involved in a deep conversation. Al stood up and pulled out two chairs for them at the table. "Jes' in time. We're havin' us a few nibbles. I'll grab ya' some wine."

DeeDee stared at the table in surprise. A mouth-watering selection of conch and lobster fritters was laid out to tempt them. "I'm not really hungry after lunch, but I'm not sure I can resist trying a conch fritter. This is a first for me." She popped one in her mouth. "Mmm, delicious." She sat down beside Jake and said, "Since when did you two learn how to rustle up such a feast?"

"When I was at Nicky's earlier, Sharisha was clearing out Nicky's fridge," Jake said as he gave her a sheepish smile. "She insisted I bring everything back here, or it would all go to waste. Chandice put the platter together for us before she went home. And there's more——tuna steaks and lobster tails for dinner. Al's going to fire up the grill for dinner, so there's nothing for you two to do. We'll take care of everything."

"Lobster, twice in one day?" Cassie half-laughed, half-groaned. "It's a tough life, but I suppose we can struggle through, can't we DeeDee?"

"You bet," DeeDee said as she accepted the glass of wine being offered to her by Al. "Thanks, Al. Sorry we're a little late getting back, but we took a bit of a detour on the way home. We saw Devan Parker at lunchtime and decided to follow her after she finished work for the day."

Jake raised an eyebrow and exchanged a look with Al before turning back to his wife. "You did, did you? I thought we'd been over this before. You know, not going after persons of interest in a murder case without running it past me first?"

DeeDee's face flushed, and before she could reply, Cassie intervened. "Jake, we didn't even get out of the car to speak to her. The driver followed at a safe distance. So safe, in fact, that we nearly lost her. For once, I wished Harry the Hatchet was behind the wheel." Harry was a friend of Al's, and a kamikaze style of driver to boot.

"Anyway, when we got to her house another woman arrived at the same time. Since we couldn't speak to Devan alone, we thought it would be better to let you guys know where she lived, and you could take it from there."

"I think I owe you an apology, DeeDee." Jake placed his hand over hers. "That was a good idea."

"I agree. Well done," Al said as he crunched on a fritter. "What have you got to show for your day, Jake, apart from all the delicious food you brought home from Nicky's place?"

Jake took a gulp of his beer. "I went through more of the security camera footage, but it didn't turn up anything. Besides Lady Gwendolyn and Devan, there were no other regular visitors to the house apart from the staff. What's bugging me, though, is why Nicky had the cameras turned off on certain days. Like Al said, I think there was something else going on that he didn't want people to see."

"Most likely business related," Al said. "I wouldn't be surprised if some of the people Nicky associated with made it a condition of meeting at his house that there were no live recording devices."

"Who could that be, Al?" DeeDee asked as she turned and stared at him. "I mean, we know Jevaun worked with him and Jevaun's on tape several times, coming and going from the jetty. It doesn't seem like he was trying to hide those meetings. Do you think Nicky was involved in something else?"

Al nodded. "Yeah, I do, but I'm not sure what. Switchin' the camera off every now and then would be a sloppy thing to do, at least from a security perspective, and believe me, there was nothin' sloppy about Nicky. He was trained the same as me. Always cover your tracks. I reckon whatever else he was hidin' could be the key to findin' his killer."

"Just a second." Jake stood up. "There's one person I think we can rule out. Back in a moment." He returned from the house with a copy of that day's Caymanian Times.

"Look," he said, opening the newspaper and spreading it out on the table. He turned several pages before stopping. "I was doing the crossword puzzle, and guess who I saw staring back at me?"

He pointed to the page with the partially completed puzzle. Underneath the crossword puzzle was a photograph of a group of women with a fine-haired blond in the middle. "That's Lady Gwendolyn Blackwood," he said, scanning the article. "And it says here she was one of the main benefactors of the charity event held at the Kimpton Seafire Resort Saturday night, where, and I'm quoting. 'cocktails were served at 5:00 p.m. and the fun continued into the early hours of the morning. Lady Blackwood was there to ensure that the fireworks went off with a bang at 8:00 p.m. The organizers would like to thank...' yada."

"Her alibi checks out, in that case," Al said. He lazed back in his seat. "Someone else we can remove from the list of suspects is Benny Amato. Detective Superintendent Watts was very helpful when I dropped by to see him this morning. He's also appreciative of our assistance, by the way. Apparently Benny's been under surveillance by the authorities for some time, which is why he was detained at the airport on arrival, just like Benny said he was." He reached for another fritter. "But here's the kicker…"

They were hanging on Al's words, waiting for him to finish chomping on his fritter. He swallowed and continued. "Now, bear in mind the police didn't tell me this, Bob Ennis did. After the cops came to Nicky's home to investigate his murder, they seized the boat that was docked at Nicky's jetty. Turns out there was illegal cargo on board. Bob was questioned for many hours about the cargo by the police yesterday, which is why I couldn't get a hold of him."

Jake exhaled. "Does Benny know? As Nicky's business partner, I guess he's implicated concerning the illegal cargo on the boat."

"Yeah, he knows," Al chuckled. "I stopped by the Grand Cayman Marriott Beach Resort this afternoon and found how he'd already checked out of the hotel. I wouldn't be surprised if the cops aren't waitin' at the airport for him, but it won't do them no good. I'm sure Benny's probably halfway to Cuba on a boat by now."

"What else did Bob Ennis have to say?" It was DeeDee's turn to speak.

Al thought for a few seconds. "Thing about Bob is, he's very loyal to Nicky, and rightfully so. Says he denied all knowledge of the cargo to the police, which is fair enough. He was only actin' on orders. With Benny gone, and Nicky dead, that's the end of it unless the police make the connection with Jevaun Henriques.

"It was Jevaun who supplied the illegal cargo, and he was supposed to be shipping it to the States once Nicky had checked it over. Nicky wanted to speak to Jevaun that night because a previous shipment had gone missin'. There was a question about whether or not Jevaun was involved."

"Sounds like if the police do make the connection, and they might have done it already, I wouldn't like to be in Jevaun's shoes," Jake said.

"So, let me see if I've got this straight," Cassie said. "Nicky and Benny were involved in a dispute with Jevaun about a missing shipment of … something we'd rather not know about. That's why Benny was here, right?"

"Yeah." Al nodded. "Benny wanted to get to the bottom of it and find out if Nicky was involved in some way. Thing is, if Benny was plannin' a hit on Nicky because of that, and I wouldn't be surprised if he was, someone else beat him to it."

DeeDee's head was spinning. "Let's go back to Jevaun. Now I understand why Nicky wanted to speak to him on Saturday. Jevaun's motive's a lot clearer. If he did try and pull a fast one on Nicky and Benny, he would have been in a lot of trouble if they ever found out, right?"

"Yeah," Al said. "Dead man walkin' kinda trouble. And accordin' to Bob, Jevaun's story about the missin' shipment doesn't stack up. Bob thinks he's lyin'." He turned to Jake. "Which is why you an' me gonna pay Jevaun a visit tomorrow. First, though, Bob's gonna' take us out on one of Nicky's boats for a tour around the island in the mornin'."

Red came wandering up to the table, and Al ran his hand over his silken coat. "You can come too, Red." He grinned. "Now that you're a seasoned sailor, like me."

"I'd like to look into Sir Alec Blackwood, Lady Gwendolyn's husband," Jake said. He gave them a recap of Sir Alec's reaction when he'd visited the Blackwood residence the previous day. "He said he'd never met Nicky, but if he was aware his wife was cheating on him with Nicky, then who knows what he'd be capable of?"

"That just leaves Devan Parker," DeeDee reminded them. "I don't see why Cassie and I can't go back to speak to her if we bring Red with us and keep in touch with you two the whole time."

"Okay, let's sleep on that one," Jake conceded. "Al, tell DeeDee and Cassie the story about how you, Nicky, and Benny first met. I think they'd enjoy it."

Al sat forward, his eyes glistening. "Right, ya' gotta' remember we were kids, ya' know? Even though I thought Benny mighta' shot me yesterday, doesn't mean we ain't buddies. That's jes' how we roll. Anyway, this one time, me and Vinny saw a young boy stealin' from a little old lady.

"She was a sweet old thing, or so we thought. Course, we chased after the kid to make him give the money back to her. I think it was a coupla' bucks, but I can't remember exactly. Guess who the kid was?"

"Nicky," they all said in unison.

"That's right." Al gave them a cheesy grin. "Well done. And guess who was waitin' around the corner when we went after Nicky?"

"Benny," came the chorus.

"Very good." Al leaned in. "We marched 'em back to where the old dame was wheelin' her shoppin' cart up an alley. So, Nicky hands her back the money and mumbles somethin' about bein' sorry an' all that. Next thing we know, the old lady punches him in the face, whips out a gun and starts shootin' all around the place. Lucky for us, she was half blind.

"Lemme' tell ya', we high-tailed it outta' there in no seconds flat. We musta' laughed for days, and after that we was friends for life. Never helped another ol' lady for a long time, mind you." He chuckled and reached in his pocket to get a handkerchief to wipe away the tears of sadness in his eyes as he thought of his lifelong friend, Nicky.

Cassie reached across the table and squeezed his hand. "I'm sure Nicky's still laughing about that one, wherever he is."

DeeDee nudged Jake, and they stood up. "We'll go get the things for dinner," she said softly.

They retreated, leaving Al, with support from his wife, Cassie, to grieve in private.

# CHAPTER FIFTEEN

The following morning, DeeDee was the last of the group to climb aboard the Princess Leia catamaran which was docked at the jetty behind Nicky's house. Bob Ennis held her arm firmly by the wrist, so she didn't lose her footing as she got on the boat.

"Hello, I'm Bob. Welcome aboard," he said, tipping his white-peaked cap, before introducing them to the rest of the crew.

First, Bob gave them a tour of the interior. They made their way past the lounge chairs and the plunge pool on the lower deck, and then they walked into a lounge and bedroom area fitted out with walnut cabinets, and leather bench seating around the perimeter. Doors at the end led to a small fully-equipped kitchen and a luxury bathroom.

Breakfast was laid out on the upper deck, which had a half-canopy to protect them from the sun. The cook had prepared a buffet appealing to every palette. Freshly squeezed juices, exotic fruits, cold meats, cheeses, pastries, muffins, crisp bacon, scrambled and poached eggs, blueberry pancakes, and Banana Bread French Toast all competed for a place in their stomachs.

Al and Jake did their best to sample a little bit of everything, although DeeDee and Cassie declared themselves defeated after two trips to the buffet table.

As the Princess Leia rounded West Bay heading towards North Sound, Bob pointed out the Marine Park. Despite the early hour, it was already swarming with divers. "You have to go on an authorized boat, if you want to dive," Bob told them. He pointed towards some sand bars visible in the distance. "That's Stingray City, where the rays are almost tame. Just a little further on, you can see eagle rays and sea turtles."

One look at Jake told DeeDee he was itching to get into the water. She turned and said to him, "Hopefully, Nicky's murder will be solved soon," she said, "and we can go reef swimming. Snorkeling in the shallow water is my limit, so if you want to go scuba diving, I'll watch from the boat."

Reaching the North Side of the island, their route took them past Rum Point, with its beautiful stretch of gleaming pearl-white sand beach. On the shore of Rum Point's sparkling clear water, exclusive million-dollar homes stood alongside more affordable condos.

"The North Side is a beautiful and historical part of the Island," Bob explained to them. They continued to cruise along the coastline at a sedate pace, past the Babylon diving site with its towering coral structure, the Pedro St. James' Castle in Pedro, the Queen Elizabeth II Botanic Park in Frank Sound, and the Wreck of the Ten Sails in Gun Bay.

"The island is around twenty-two miles long, and four miles wide," Bob informed them. "Not big at all. But there's enough to see and do on it to keep anyone busy here for a long time. In the morning, on cruise ship days, it can get really busy in George Town and Stingray City, but by the afternoon most of the tourists are heading back to their cruise ships and it quiets down again."

DeeDee closed her eyes, forgetting about Nicky's murder for just long enough to absorb the feeling of floating in paradise. If someone had told her she and Jake could never leave, it would have been okay with her, provided her children could come and visit occasionally. The conversation Al was having with Bob brought her back to her surroundings.

"Bob, me and Jake are gonna' pay a visit to Jevaun Henriques after we get back to Nicky's. Do you know where he lives?'

Out of one eye, DeeDee watched Bob make his way across the deck to sit beside Al.

"Sure," Bob said. "There's a community of Rastafarians that live just outside of George Town. Jevaun's a true believer in Rasta, and he's much looked up to by the people in the community. He lives in a large family compound located in the community. Just ask for him when you get there. Everyone knows him."

He gave Al some directions as Al nodded and said, "Uh-huh," a couple of times. "Got it, thanks Bob."

Returning to Nicky's before lunchtime, they thanked Bob and the crew for the tour and walked the short distance back to Al and Cassie's home.

"I think we oughta' go straight to look for Jevaun," Al said to Jake, beeping the key fob for his Lamborghini as they walked up the driveway. "Cassie an' DeeDee, ain't no point ya' goin' to Devan's until she's finished work. Let's keep in touch, and if me an' Jake aren't back before ya' leave, let us know your whereabouts at all times, got it?"

The two women nodded affirmatively.

Jake embraced DeeDee. "Please be careful. Make sure you've got Red, your phone, and the driver in close proximity, whatever happens. Deal?"

"Pinky promise," DeeDee said, brushing her lips against his. "Go, we'll be fine. And if you find out that Jevaun's the murderer before we leave to meet with Devan, we won't have to go farther than the beach all afternoon. As far as I'm concerned, that would be the best result."

Jake gave her a tight smile. "If only things were that simple and straightforward, but let's hope you're right."

*****

Bob's directions were better than the ones Teddy had given to Jake a couple of days earlier, plus Al knew his way around the island fairly well. As a result, it didn't take long to reach the Rastafarian community Bob had described.

Looking around, Jake could tell they were among 'yard' Rastas, the more radical Rastafarian sect. Many of the people they saw wore their hair in dreadlocks and were dressed in the colors of Rastafarianism, red for the blood to be shed for their redemption and freedom, green for the vegetation of the motherland, black for their race, and gold, representing the wealth of the homeland, Africa.

Al parked his car and when they climbed out, he motioned to a young boy standing in the street. "Here, kid. Ya' wanna' make twenty bucks?"

The boy came over and stopped several paces away. "What do I have to do?"

Al pulled a roll of bills from his pocket. Licking his thumb, he peeled off a twenty-dollar bill. "Stand here and take care of my car. No one touches it, not even you, okay?'

The boy nodded and held out his hand.

Al slapped the twenty in his palm. "There'll be another one for ya' when I get back, so long as there's not even a thumbprint on it, ya' hear me?"

"Loud and clear," the boy said, folding the note carefully and sticking it in a pocket of his long combat shorts.

"Ya' know where we can find Jevaun Henriques?" Al asked him.

"Maybe."

Al sighed and handed him another twenty.

This time, the boy grinned. "Try the community hall," he said, pointing at the building across the street from where they were standing. The door was open, and various people were coming and going.

"Thanks, kid."

Jake followed Al across the street. Inside the hall, it took a few seconds for his eyes to adjust to the relative darkness of its interior compared to the bright sunlight they had just left behind. A smell hit him, the smell of cannabis, or ganja, as it was known locally. People milled around, and although he couldn't see anyone openly smoking, he got the impression it wouldn't be a problem if anyone did. Reggae music played in the background. The vibe was chilled, and not at all threatening, even when Jake realized they were the only non-Rasta people present in the large room.

"Good afternoon." A middle-aged man appeared beside them and addressed them with a polite nod. "My name is Zion Kelly, one of the elders in our community. We welcome all denominations here, all except trouble, that is. How may I help you, gentlemen?"

Al introduced himself and Jake. "We're lookin' for Jevaun Henriques. Is he here?"

Zion shook his head. "Not at the moment, although he may be along later. Is he…is he in some kind of trouble?"

"We're investigatin' the murder of Nicky Luchesse, a business associate of his," Al went on, in a low voice. "Ya' might have heard about it? We were wonderin' if anyone saw Jevaun or knows where he was around the time it happened on Saturday evenin'."

Zion's expression gave nothing away. "Please, follow me," he said, leading them into a side room that looked like it doubled as a kitchen as well as an office. Several chairs were scattered around. "Take a seat," Zion said, waiting until they were settled before sitting himself.

"I heard about Mr. Luchesse," Zion continued, in a thoughtful manner. "News like that travels fast on a small island. I'm not sure how Jevaun could have been involved, since he was here on Saturday afternoon and stayed here until late that night. The community was gathered to observe the religious festival of the Crowning of Emperor Haile Selassie I."

"Hmm," Al said, rubbing his chin. "We kinda' need to know what time he arrived, 'cuz a frienda' mine by the name of Bob Ennis said he spoke to Jevaun around 4:00 p.m. Jevaun was supposed to be on his way to meet him at Nicky's place. For all we know, Jevaun mighta' gone there first, before comin' here. Ain't that right, Jake?"

Jake nodded, his eyes never leaving Zion's.

"One moment, gentlemen," Zion said, getting up. "I'll be right back."

"Whaddya think?" Al hissed at Jake after Zion left the room. "Cool customer, huh?"

"I don't think he's hiding anything," Jake said. "But let's wait and see what he comes up with."

Zion returned holding a heavy hard-covered book. He handed it to Al. "This is the community book of observance. You'll see it covers a lot of different holy days, with November 2 being the most recent. The sign-in and sign-out times are marked in the book. We need the times for fire regulations purposes, in case we need to evacuate the building and account for people. I have no idea what time Mr. Luchesse was killed, but the book shows what time Jevaun arrived and when he left."

"Could we borrow this, do ya' think?" Al asked as he flicked through the pages. He wanted to take a closer look at it and show it to the police if necessary.

"No problem. You said you had a couple of questions, Mr De Duco. What was the other one?"

Al cracked his knuckles. "Seems like there was a dispute between Mr. Henriques and Mr. Luchesse about a valuable shipment goin' missin.' Do ya' know any reason why Jevaun would lie about that, money problems, for example?"

Zion stared at Al, his gaze unblinking. "Can't say as I do." He forced a smile. "If that's all, I'll see you out. Keep the book for as long as you need it. We have nothing to hide here."

"Thanks, Zion," Al said as he and Jake shook his hand and let him lead them to the main exit.

Jake felt Zion's eyes on them from where the elder remained standing in the doorway watching them cross the street to Al's car. A small crowd of children had gathered around the roadster, its juvenile guard making sure no one stepped too close. When Al and Jake approached, the children scrambled away in all directions.

"Thanks, kid," Al said, handing him a bundle of cash. "Ya' done good."

With a delighted grin, the boy ran away, stuffing the money in his pocket.

"What time does the book say Jevaun was there on Saturday?" Al asked Jake as he drove off with tires screeching.

Jake flicked through the pages. "There were hundreds of people in attendance, so it might take me a while to find him. Oh, wait a minute, this looks like it." He held the book at arm's length. "If it's the same Jevaun Henriques, then he's signed in from just after 4:30 p.m. Saturday until he left at midnight. In which case, he might have been intending on meeting Bob at Nicky's place, but something made him change his mind and come to the community instead."

"Maybe he wanted to pray for his sins," Al said. "I got the impression Zion knew more than he was lettin' on about my second question."

"I agree," Jake said. "But if Jevaun was at the community during the time in question, it's irrelevant."

"True." Al scratched his head. "Let's take that book to the police department and see if Detective Superintendent Watts has come up with anythin'. I'm hopin' he has, cuz' we sure as heck ain't findin' nothin'."

# CHAPTER SIXTEEN

At the George Town Police Station, Al sighed and turned to Jake. "I guess we should have checked to see if Detective Superintendent Watts was available before we came over. Ain't nothin' we can do till he comes back from his meetin'. Whaddya' say we grab some lunch and come back later?"

Jake thought for a moment. "Sure. Or we could pay a call on Sir Alec Blackwood and get something to eat on the way. After our breakfast of kings, a snack will keep me going for now."

"Sounds like a plan." Al was already striding out of the police station with Jake right behind him.

Once they were out of George Town, Al drove in the direction of Pease Bay. They stopped at a roadside cafe for coffee and sandwiches to go and then pulled into a beach parking lot to enjoy the view of the breakers as they ate.

"What do we know about Sir Alec?" Al asked, when they set off on the last leg of the trip to the manor house.

"From what I've been able to find out online and from speaking to Teddy and Chandice," Jake said, "the Blackwoods have had a family presence on Grand Cayman for several hundred years. Sir Alec is an only child and spent much of his childhood in England. He went to college in the United States and has dabbled in several business ventures. The latest one sells expensive electronic toys and gaming gadgets designed for use by adults. He raised capital for the start-up from his rich friends, but the company's financials show that the venture is struggling. He runs the business out of an annex at the family home and claims a lot of tax deductions that way."

"Are his parents still on the scene?"

Jake shook his head. "Both dead. Teddy told me Sir Alec's father killed himself more than twenty years ago. He blew his brains out with a shotgun."

Al winced. "Ew."

"The mother moved back to England and remarried but has since passed away. Sir Alec took over the family property and investments after his parents died. The investments were badly managed, and word has it the only thing of value left is the land the home is built on. When you see the state of the crumbling old house, you'll understand."

Al turned into the narrow driveway, driving at a snail's pace to get a good look at the house and grounds. "I see what ya' mean. The lawn could do with some new sod and waterin', for starters. It's pretty impressive, all the same. Shame the house is so decrepit. It looks haunted."

"That's the problem with old money," Jake said. "There's only so much of it."

Al pulled to a stop at the front of the house, and they got out. The Bentley was there, but there was no sign of the Jaguar. At the top of the steps, Jake rapped the lion's head door knocker against the door. Moments later, it was opened by the maid.

"Hello, Marla." Jake remembered her name from his visit to see Lady Gwendolyn. "We're here to see Mr. Blackwood. It's Al De Duco, and Ja—"

Marla cut him off. "Yes, I remember. Sir Alec is in his office. There is a separate entrance around the back of the house. His receptionist will look after you." With a nod, she shut the door with a thump.

"Charmin'," Al muttered. "She's a cranky ol' battle-axe, that's fer sure."

Patchy gravel crunched underfoot as they walked around the side of the house towards the back. There, an open grassy area the size of a football field was littered with toys of various shapes and sizes, mainly battery operated helicopters, cars, and planes.

Jutting out from the back of the house was a modern building addition with blinds on the windows, and a door with a sign above it that read 'Toyz for Boyz.'

Al gave Jake a sideways look. "This should be interestin.'"

They were greeted by a bubbly receptionist who introduced herself as Betty. "Hello, may I help you?" she asked with an English accent.

"We don't have an appointment," Jake said, "but if Sir Alec can spare a few minutes, we'd like a quick word with him."

"He's outside playing with his drones. I'll fetch you some tea, and then I'll let him know you're here."

"We could just go out and find him," Al suggested.

"Oh no, sir. I have to make everyone tea. Sir Alec gets mad if I don't. And cake, of course."

Al grinned. "Tea and cake. That's fine by us, isn't it Jake?"

"Definitely." Jake motioned towards some comfy leather reclining seats, and they sat down.

The reception area resembled a man cave, with a jukebox in one corner and a pool table stretching the length of one side of the room. A big screen playing a Steve McQueen movie was fixed on a wall, and slouchy technicolor bean bags were positioned around the room. Gaming devices and headsets were scattered here and there. Jake flipped up the armrest of his recliner to reveal a mini-fridge stocked with beer, chocolate, and gummy bears.

"Oh boy," Al said, his eyes lighting up. "Jake, I think we're in the wrong business." He stretched out his palm. "C'mon, gimme a gummy bear or three." He put a pair of thick goggles over his eyes, and let out a grunt, tearing them off again. "What the—?"

"It's a virtual reality headset," Jake said knowingly. "I've heard they're amazing."

Al rolled his eyes and picked up an iPad instead. "At least I know what this is. Cassie has one."

They were interrupted by Betty returning with the tea and cake. The tea was served in delicate china cups and the cake came on its own stand. Sprinkled with powdered sugar, in between two layers of plain sponge cake was a layer of whipped cream and strawberries.

"We definitely need to up our office game," Al muttered, spilling a few crumbs between bites. "Starbucks takeout ain't gonna cut it after this."

"Gentlemen." Sir Alec entered from outside, smoothing down his thinning hair. His eyes narrowed when he recognized Jake, and he skipped any introductions. "Please, follow, me. Do bring your tea." He waved his arm at Betty. "Earl Grey for me. And shortbread."

Betty hurried off.

Sir Alec led them through a door into the older part of the house, where the hallway was paneled with thick dark wood. There were no family portraits in this part of the hallway, just several mismatched rugs covering the cold stone floor. The hallway led them to Sir Alec's office. Its walls were lined with bookshelves, and against one was a large glass cabinet containing shotguns and pistols of various shapes and sizes.

Sir Alec saw Al scrutinizing the guns. "Do you ever hunt? It's an English tradition you know, although it's banned now." He shrugged. "Doesn't stop us, though."

Al shook his head. "Can't say as I do. Seems cruel to me, killin' innocent animals fer no reason. Quite a collection of guns you've got there, all the same." He sat down without waiting to be asked, and Jake followed suit.

Sir Alec went to the other side of his desk, sat down and steepled his fingers, resting his elbows on the table. Apart from when Betty brought in Sir Alec's tea, there was silence as the men faced off against each other.

Al spoke first. "We'll get straight to the point, Sir Alec, cuz' ya' must be a busy man."

Sir Alec nodded, straightening up in his seat.

"As ya' know from meetin' Jake already, we're investigatin' the death of Nicky Luchesse," Al said. "Could ya' tell us where ya' were Saturday afternoon, between 5:00 p.m. and 8:00 p.m.?"

A slow smile spread across Sir Alec's face. "I was at the Ritz-Carlton Golf Club, where you'll always find me on a Saturday. I played nine holes with my lawyer, Freddie Jackson, teeing off at 3:00 p.m. After the game, we had a couple of drinks in the bar and then decided to stay for dinner. My wife was out for the evening, and I don't like to dine alone."

"What time did you leave the Ritz-Carlton, Sir Alec?" Jake asked him.

"Around 10:00 p.m. I remember, because when Freddie realized how late it was he said he would be in trouble with his wife if he didn't get home soon." He smirked and took a sip of his tea.

"What about you, Sir Alec, does your wife not mind if you're home late?" Al's eyes narrowed as he spoke. "I know if it was my wife she'd be worried if I was gone all day and hadn't called her."

Jake turned to Al. "But your wife's not having an affair. Unlike Sir Alec's."

Sir Alec banged the desk. "How dare you," he said, his face reddening. "The state of my marriage is none of your business."

Al shook his head. "It is, when your wife was sleeping with the victim of a murder, Sir Alec. Seems to me, that would give ya' a pretty good motive to kill him."

Sir Alec choked ever so slightly on his tea. "The first I knew about my wife's dalliance with Mr. Luchesse was after Mr. Rogers' visit here on Sunday." He glared pointedly at Jake. "After he left I confronted my wife about it, and Gwen told me everything about her sordid affair with Mr. Luchesse. Although she made a terrible error of judgement, the way Mr. Luchesse treated her was appalling. If he was still alive, I'd have a few sharp words for him. As it is, my wife and I have decided to put this behind us and work on healing our marriage."

"Ain't that sweet. Where's the violin music when ya' need it, huh?" Al lurched across the desk pointing his finger at Sir Alec and causing him to shrink back. "Are ya' tellin' me, ya' didn't know Nicky Luchesse was carryin' on with yer' wife before he died?"

"I am."

"Did ya', or did ya' not, Sir Alec, have any other dealings with Nicky Luchesse, on any matter whatsoever?"

"I did not."

"And can Mr. Freddie Jackson vouch for your whereabouts from

3:00 p.m. Saturday until 10:00 p.m.?"

"He can."

"Fine." Al stood up. "If you're lyin', Sir Alec, Ima gonna' come after ya', and hunt ya' down, until justice has been done. Do I make myself clear?"

"Crystal."

Al shook his head. "C'mon, Jake. I smell smoke. Someone's pants are on fire. Let's go."

Jake nodded at Sir Alec and followed Al out.

Walking back through the reception area, Al was charm personified. "Thanks fer the tea, Betty. Have a great day." It wasn't until he was outside that he turned the air blue.

They marched back to the car with Al thinking aloud. "Jake, we gotta' speak to Freddie Jackson, find out if what Sir Alec's sayin' is true. Sir Alec's a weasel, as far as I can see, and I wouldn't be surprised if he's our man."

"Sure, I can do that." Jake scratched his head. "I still think there's something we're missing. Some other angle we haven't thought of."

"Yeah, I hear ya'. Maybe Detective Superintendent Watts can help us put the pieces together. Next stop George Town. You can find Freddie Jackson's office, and talk to him while I go back to the police station."

On the way down the driveway, Al pulled over to let a large Mercedes drive past. "That must be Sir Alec's next appointment," he said, nodding at the other driver. A second man, dressed in dark clothing, sat in the passenger seat.

"Do you know them?" Jake asked, looking back. "One of the men waved to you like he knew you."

Al screwed up his face. "Maybe, I can't place him. He mighta' waved cuz' I pulled over to let him get past me on the narrow driveway. Or, it could be someone I've had a drink with at Calico Jack's. It'll come to me."

# CHAPTER SEVENTEEN

On his way to the police station, Al dropped Jake off in the center of George Town.

"I'll call you after I've talked to Freddie Jackson," Jake said, climbing out of Al's roadster. "I just need to find him first."

A couple of pedestrians crossed the street in front of Al's car, and Al revved the engine, making them jump. He grinned at them before turning back to Jake. "Gotcha. Ima gonna' keep chasin' after Detective Superintendent Watts until he talks to me. By the way, where did ya' put that book the Rasta guy gave us?" He glanced around the car. "I don't see it. Hope it ain't gone walkin'."

"In the glove compartment," Jake said.

He watched Al speed off before making his way to a nearby coffee shop. Inside, he made the mistake of ordering and paying for an espresso and a bottle of water before realizing air conditioning wasn't part of the deal.

He stayed in the muggy coffee shop just long enough to do an internet search for Freddie Jackson and to discover his law firm was located in the business district, just a ten-minute walk away. Gulping down his espresso and armed with his water and Google Maps on his phone, he set off through the bustling streets filled with shoppers and workers and headed towards the Jackson Law Office.

Jake didn't pay much attention to the shopping area, apart from noticing there were several duty-free shopping malls, and in general the stores seemed to be catering to affluent customers. As he neared the business and financial district, the prosperity of the area was apparent among the well-heeled professionals walking around with phones glued to their ears.

Al had told him the main line of work on Grand Cayman was not fishing or tourism, but financial services. As a tax haven and international financial center, it was home to over one hundred thousand registered companies, most of them only visible on paper. That meant a lot of accountants and lawyers were squirreled away in the glass buildings such as the one he found himself entering. Freddie Jackson was one of them.

A ding signaled his arrival on the 10th floor, where the Jackson Law reception desk faced him when he stepped out of the elevator.

"Hello, would it be possible to see Mr. Jackson, please? I'm not a client. It's in connection with a friend of his, Sir Alec Blackwood. My name is Jake Rogers."

The receptionist smiled. "Mr. Jackson is expecting you, sir." She stood up and pointed her hand down a nearby corridor. "His office is at the end, third door on the left."

"Thank you." The reason Jake hadn't phoned ahead was he had been hoping for an element of surprise. He surmised the only explanation for Freddie expecting his visit was that Sir Alec himself had called Freddie to tip him off.

*What does Sir Alec have to hide?* Jake thought to himself.

He didn't have to wait long to try and find out. Freddie Jackson met him at the door of his office and welcomed him with a friendly handshake. "Come on in, Jake," he said, leading him to a small conference table with a view from the floor-to-ceiling window of numerous other nearby office buildings. "Coffee, tea, scotch?"

"No thanks, Freddie." Jake sat down opposite Freddie. "I take it Sir Alec told you about our meeting with him earlier?"

"He did. I'm his lawyer as well as his friend, so I'm interested in any allegations being thrown around about him. I should warn you, Sir Alec takes his good name very seriously and won't hesitate to sue for monetary damages if there's any hint of slander."

"I understand. So far, Sir Alec's not being accused of anything. My colleague, Al De Duco, and I are currently helping the local police with their investigation into the murder of Nicky Luchesse."

"I see, but I'm not sure what that has to do with Sir Alec."

"Sir Alec's wife was having an affair with Mr. Luchesse. We believe that establishes a motive why he may have been involved with the crime."

"Hmm." Freddie gazed at a spot behind Jake's head, avoiding any eye contact with Jake. If he was surprised by the news of Lady Gwendolyn's affair, he didn't show it. He seemed deep in thought.

Jake pressed him. "Can you confirm Sir Alec's whereabouts on Saturday? He said he was with you."

Freddie snapped back into the moment. "That's right. He was with me. We played golf at the Ritz-Carlton Golf Club at 3:00 p.m. and had drinks and dinner afterwards. I left him at around 10:00 p.m."

Jake stared at him in dismay. As far as he could tell, Freddie's body language indicated he was telling the truth. Would a lawyer lie to protect his client? Jake very much doubted it. At least, not without a huge payoff, and Sir Alec didn't have much money.

"Did he leave you at any time, excuse himself…"

"You mean, slip away to murder someone?" Freddie shook his head. "You're grabbing at straws, Jake. Sir Alec has his problems, but he couldn't have killed Nicky Luchesse. His alibi is rock solid. The only time I wasn't by his side was when he made a phone call or sent messages on his phone. That's not unusual, I do it myself. And at all times he was within my view. In case you're wondering, I wouldn't jeopardize my career to protect a criminal."

Jake leaned forward. "You said Sir Alec has problems. What exactly did you mean?"

Freddie frowned. "I've said too much, and I'm afraid I'll have to ask you to leave. I hope you find the perpetrator." He stood up and walked to the door, holding it open.

"Thanks, Freddie, I appreciate your time." Jake said.

"You're welcome," Freddie replied as he hastily closed the door to his office, but because he was in such a hurry, he failed to close the door entirely.

Jake crouched down in the hallway next to the partially closed door on the pretext of needing to tie his shoelace. Through a crack in the door, he saw Freddie make his way to his desk and pick up the telephone.

Jake could just make out what Freddie was saying through the crack in the partially closed door.

"Sir Alec? I think we need to talk."

*****

"The town car's here," Cassie said as she picked up her purse. "Have you heard anything from Jake?"

DeeDee shook her head. "Nothing, other than a text to say he's on his way to meet Al at the police station. Where's Red?"

At the sound of his name, Red came trotting into the hallway. DeeDee spotted Holt loitering in the background. "I think Holt is still wary of me," she said, petting Red. "I thought you liked playing it cool, Red, but you're a pussycat compared to Holt." She looked up, and Holt bared his teeth before silently backing off.

"He was like that with me too, the first time I was here," Cassie said. "Don't worry, he'll be better on your next visit."

"That sounds promising." DeeDee straightened up. "We get to come again?"

Cassie opened the front door. "Of course, you do. A murder investigation's not a proper holiday. Next time, no murders."

They had the same driver as they'd had the day before. He transported them to Devan's apartment in Bodden Town which was only thirty minutes away. Situated beside the beach, the area was mostly residential, and had the classic feel of a small Caribbean town.

"I'm texting Jake to let him know we're here," DeeDee said, tapping the screen of her phone.

Before they climbed out of the town car, they agreed in advance with the driver that he would wait outside with the engine running for the duration of their visit.

"We'll bring Red in with us, and if we're not back in fifteen minutes, can you knock on the door and come and get us, please?" Cassie asked him.

The driver looked dubious. "I don't know what this is about, ma'am, but I don't want any trouble."

Cassie nodded. "Neither do we. In that case, if we're not back in fifteen minutes, call the police."

That settled, Cassie, DeeDee and Red approached the apartment. It was on ground level, with another apartment on the level above.

The apartment building was well-maintained with a landscaped garden in the front area.

DeeDee rang the bell, and the door was opened by a woman in her early twenties. DeeDee recognized the family similarity, but this woman wasn't Devan. She was pretty, but not beautiful.

"Hello," DeeDee said. "We're looking for Devan Parker, is she home?"

The woman beamed at them "No, I'm her sister, Naomi, would you like to come in and I'll write down your name and phone number and give it to her when she returns?" She glanced down, and when she saw Red, she froze and took a step back.

"It's okay, he won't bite unless there's a threat," Cassie said. "He's well-trained."

"It's not that, I'm allergic to dogs."

Cassie whispered a command to Red, and he walked several paces away and laid down on the ground, watching them.

"Is that better?" Cassie said. "We won't come in, in that case. If you could just let her know I came by. My name is Cassie De Duco. I'll leave you my number. My husband and I have a vacation home on the island, and someone my husband trusts recommended Devan as an excellent private banking consultant. My friend here and I were out for a drive, and I heard Devan lived here so, um…" Cassie's voice trailed off.

"I don't understand why you didn't make an appointment to see her at the bank," Naomi said.

"I'm sorry, I shouldn't have come," Cassie said. "This was a crazy idea. It's just that we've had a bad experience before, and some money was stolen by a banking officer who diverted it to their own account. Sometimes you can tell by someone's home circumstances whether something like that is more likely to apply. It obviously doesn't apply here, so please accept my apologies."

"That's okay, I've heard of that happening too," Naomi said. A telephone sounded in the background, and she added, "I need to get that. If you want to write down your number, I'll give it to Devan when she comes home."

DeeDee reached inside her purse and handed Cassie a pen and a piece of paper from the notebook she always carried with her. Cassie wrote out her number on the page and handed it to Naomi when she returned.

"Thanks," Naomi said. "That was Devan on the phone. She won't be home tonight, since she has a date with her new boyfriend. But she said she'll get back to you as soon as possible."

"That sounds exciting," DeeDee said, surprised. *Maybe Nicky wasn't the only one seeing Devan,* she thought. "Is it someone she just met?"

Naomi smiled. "No, weirdly enough she's known him for ages. It's her boss. She absolutely detested him until they suddenly got together two weeks ago. Now, she's fallen head over heels in love with him. I haven't seen her in days. I don't think they can bear to be apart. She spends all day with him at the bank and then all night with him at his apartment. She's only been home to pick up a few things, and then she disappears back into her love bubble."

"Aw, that's cute." Cassie smiled at Naomi. "It was really nice to meet you, and I hope to meet Devan soon."

"Bye," DeeDee said as Naomi shut the door.

"Come on, Red," Cassie said, patting her leg. "Time to go."

When they returned to the car, DeeDee spoke up and said, "I guess I'd better let Jake know we can strike Devan off the suspect list. She's been with her boss, and now boyfriend, around the clock for the past few days. Another dead end."

# CHAPTER EIGHTEEN

Al was pacing in the police station parking lot next to his car when Jake met him after visiting Freddie Jackson. "Well, can we nail Sir Alec?" Al asked him.

Jake shook his head, indicating the answer was no.

"Get in the car and tell me what went down," Al said with a grimace. "Then I'll fill ya' in on the info I got from the cops."

When Jake had brought him up to speed on his meeting with Freddie, including the critical fact that Sir Alec had been with Freddie almost the entire day Nicky was murdered, Al banged the steering wheel with his fist. "Darn, that weasel Blackwood. Ima sure he's lyin', especially after what Detective Superintendent Watts told me about the weapon that killed Nicky."

"Your turn,' Jake said. "What did Watts say?"

"First off, let me tell ya' about Jevaun Henriques. Turns out the cops have been watchin' him and Nicky for quite a while. They probably woulda' got busted if Nicky hadn't been bumped off. The police ain't got nothin' on Jevaun because all the candy was on Nicky's boat."

"That explains why Benny got hauled in at the airport," Jake said.

"That's right. Meantime, Benny's gone AWOL and won't be showin' his face around here for a long time. As far as Nicky's murder goes, Jevaun's in the clear. He was under 24 hour around the clock surveillance by the cops. Some police officer by the name of Johnson can vouch for Jevaun being at his community compound the whole time in question on Saturday. Detective Superintendent Watts said they could investigate how Jevaun financed his lifestyle and try and pin somethin' on him that way, but that could take years."

Jake's phone buzzed, and he pulled it out of his pocket. "It's a message from DeeDee," he said, scrolling down the screen. "They're just leaving Devan Parker's place." He looked sideways at Al. "They turned up nothing on her either."

"Dang. Okay, back to Nicky. The police were able to tell me Nicky was killed with a .50 caliber bullet, probably from a Smith & Wesson Model 500."

"Whoa." Jake turned to him in surprise. "That's some serious piece of hardware."

Al nodded. "Exactly. Which brings us full circle to Sir Alec Blackwood. I was tryin' to remember if I saw an S&W pistol in his gun cabinet, but I'm pretty sure I didn't. The weird thing is, the only person I know with one of those guns was Nicky. He showed it to me when he got it not that long ago. I was askin' him where to buy a piece like that around here, but he wouldn't spill. It was like he wanted to keep it a secret from me which doesn't make much sense cuz' we was lifelong friends."

"Is Nicky's gun still at his place?"

"Yep. That was one of the things I checked when I found him. I know where he keeps it, and it hadn't been used."

Jake's brow was furrowed. "Seems like we're close to something, but not close enough. Let's suppose whoever shot Nicky got their gun from the same source Nicky got his. Does that sound reasonable?"

Al's eyes lit up, and a grin spread across his face from ear to ear. "Oh, boy. Now yer' talkin'." He slapped his forehead with the palm of his hand and started the car's engine. "Let's go. One more stop, and if I'm right, we're gonna' wrap up this murder investigation."

Screeching through the George Town evening traffic at breakneck speed, Al turned to Jake. "Get Bob Ennis on the phone, will ya'? Tell him we're on the way to the marina where Nicky keeps his boats, and to meet us there, pronto. Ima gonna' wanna' see inside 'em all, and I'll break 'em open if need be. With his help, I might not have to."

"What exactly are we looking for, Al?" Jake asked as he closed his eyes for a second when a truck coming in the other direction almost wiped them out. "I think this is a one-way street, by the way," he added, "and I think you're going in the wrong direction.

"You'll see," Al muttered, swerving onto the empty sidewalk to avoid the truck. "You'll see."

Bob was waiting for them at the marina when they arrived, and Al explained what was on his mind. "Bob, this is important. I need to know if Nicky was hidin' anythin', any candy that he didn't mention to Benny, that sorta' thing. If you don't know nothin' about it, we're gonna have to search the boats. Tear 'em apart, if necessary."

Bob's jaw tightened. "Al, no. Don't touch the boats. It would break the skipper's heart. The thing is…" He hesitated, dropping his head and staring at the ground.

Al pressed him for an answer. "Go on. Bob. You've got to tell us. What was Nicky up to that he didn't want anyone to know about?"

"Nicky left me instructions. Who to call if something like this happened to him," Bob said, looking back up at Al. "I don't know what was in the other crates, but someone already picked them up."

"Other crates? Okay, lemme' get this straight. There were crates of candy on the boat that was seized by the police, right?"

Bob nodded.

"Did Nicky have a separate stash of candy that he was keepin' back?"

"Not candy, something else. Nicky kept them on different boats."

Jake could see Al was getting exasperated. "Bob," he said gently, "when were the other crates picked up?"

"Sunday, the day after Nicky was murdered. I called the number Nicky gave me right after I heard about the murder."

"And who collected them?" Jake continued. "Was it Benny?"

"No, sir. Two different men. They didn't say much, just told me they had come to collect their stuff. They had a crew who took Nicky's boats away and returned them minus the cargo." He turned to Al, his eyes pleading. "Al, I'm sorry if I acted out of turn. What else could I do?

Al's face softened. "S'ok, Bob, I understand. Ya' was followin' Nicky's orders, an' ya' done good. Can ya' describe the men in charge?"

Relief washed over Bob. "Yes, sir. Dark hair, both tall. One was dressed in black clothes, the other had a big gold watch."

Jake turned to Al. "The men we saw in the Mercedes driving into Sir Alec's place when we were leaving, right?"

Al nodded, a ray of the fading sunshine glinting off his sunglasses. "Yep. It came to me outside the police station how I knew them. Monty Malone and his sidekick Murph, international gun dealers extraordinaire. I used to do a little business with them, back in the days when I was with the Mob in Chicago. I ain't seen 'em for a long time. They musta' recognized me when we was leaving Sir Alec's and that's why they waved to me."

Al turned to Bob and shook his hand. "Bob, it's been a pleasure, but me an' Jake really gotta' run."

*****

When Jake and Al sprinted into the reception area of Sir Alec's office a little while later, Betty gave them a ditzy smile. "Hello, again. Sir Alec is expecting you."

"No, he ain't. Where is he?" Al demanded. He stalked off towards the door that led into the hallway but was halted by Betty's reply. "Sir Alec's outside, playing with his drones. I'll fetch you some tea and cake and let him know you're here."

Al swiveled around and held up his hand. "No, Betty, yer' tea and cake are delicious, really, but that's not the purpose of our little visit. We'll go outside and find him, if that's alright."

Jake followed Al onto the flat grassy area and picked up a couple of the toys strewn on the ground. A remote-control helicopter, with one of its blades warped. Another, a remote-control Lamborghini, seemed to have had a bad accident, its whole front end was crushed into a mess of warped plastic with wires hanging out. He held it up to show Al.

"Ouch," Al said. "That's how not to treat a Lambo. And that one didn't have air bags."

They made their way across the lawn and down a bank dotted with untended bushes and plants. What had once been magnificent grounds had morphed into a neglected wilderness, branches and overgrown roots blocking their descent every few feet. At the bottom of the bank was another flat area where a dried-up fountain stood forlornly in the middle, surrounded by cracked brick paving sprouting with weeds.

The sound of a buzzing noise overhead caused Jake to look up.

"Uh-oh," he said, ducking just in time to escape a headlong collision with a flying object resembling a large metallic bird with claws.

"What the—" The birdlike object circled as Al ducked down behind a bush.

"It's okay," Jake said with a chuckle. "It's a drone. Sir Alec must be nearby."

He turned around, and a grinning Sir Alec stepped into view from behind a tree. He was holding a cell phone, and a shotgun was slung over his shoulder on a strap. "There you are, at last. I was wondering how long it would take you two to show up again. I've been expecting you."

"Really?" Al stood up from his position behind the bush.

"Yes. Freddie told me Jake paid him a visit, checking my alibi. I thought it was only a matter of time before you put the rest of the puzzle pieces together. You were quicker than I thought, I'll give you credit for that."

Al stepped forward and addressed Sir Alec with a growl. "Why did ya' do it, Sir Alec? Kill Nicky, I mean. It wasn't just cuz' of him carryin' on with Lady Gwendolyn, was it?"

"Ha," Sir Alec said with a snarl. "That slimeball Luchesse must have thought I was a complete numbskull. Sleeping with my wife was bad enough, but when I found out what else he'd been up to, there was no way I could let him get away with it. Family pride, you see." In a combat maneuver, he swung the shotgun around in split second and pointed it at Al and Jake, flipping the safety catch off. "Stay where you are. Don't come any closer."

Al raised his hands in the air, and with a sideways look, Jake followed suit.

Jabbing the shotgun towards Al, Sir Alec added, "Don't try anything clever, you goon, like reaching for the gun tucked inside your pants. Or else."

"That's not very nice, callin' me a goon," Al said, clicking his tongue. "Ima not sure I like that sorta' talk. Do you, Jake?"

Jake looked at Al and then back to Sir Alec. He wasn't sure what Al had up his sleeve, but he hoped it was a gun. In any case, with a loaded shotgun pointed in his direction, he had no option but to play along. "No, Al, I don't."

Sir Alec took a step closer, matched by Al and Jake taking a step back. "Tell me, Jake," Sir Alec said, "did Freddie tell you about the Blackwood family history of madness? My father shot himself, and his father did the same before that. They heard voices, you see. I get them too. Jolly annoying, I might add."

"No, Freddie didn't say anything about that," Jake said, his voice slow and steady, hoping to calm Sir Alec down as it appeared he was becoming more and more agitated.

"That was decent of him. He's a good sport, old Freddie. I think he knew I was up to something, though." A crazed expression came over Sir Alec's face, and he began to shake his head and blink his eyes rapidly. After a moment or two, he slapped himself on the temple, and the shaking stopped. "That's the voices," he said with a forlorn smile.

"What else was Nicky involved in that upset you, Sir Alec? Was it the guns?" Al asked.

"Yes, it was the guns. I made a deal with Monty Malone and Murph, you see, to help them transport illegal guns to Mexico. I met them at a party, frightfully clever chaps." Sir Alec's eyes glazed over and again, he started blinking rapidly. "And when Freddie told me about their line of business, I realized we were the perfect fit for a mutually beneficial arrangement."

"What kinda' arrangement was that, Sir Alec?" Al asked in a smooth, polite tone of voice.

"They had an issue with the transportation arrangements for their guns."

Al chuckled. "Ya' don't say. And lemme' guess, you were gonna' help them with that through your toy distribution network for Toyz for Boyz. That's some toy, a Smith & Wesson Model 500, huh?"

"It is indeed, Al, you're right about that. Anyway, when I was informed by them that my price had been undercut by Nicky on the deal, I couldn't just let it go. What's a self-respecting person like me to do?" Sir Alec shrugged his shoulders. "The money involved would have been enough to dig me out of a rather large financial hole in which I found myself. Apparently, Nicky was going to use his luxury yachts to travel to Mexico with the guns hidden on board.

"His plan was to charter the yachts to unsuspecting wealthy travelers using his own crews. The cargo would be picked up at sea while the yachters slept, effectively negating Nicky's costs, and the reason why he was able to undercut my price by a wide margin. When Monty Malone and Murph mentioned they saw you here earlier, I had to tell them it was too late to cut me back in on the deal. It was quite clear to me I was about to be discovered."

Jake stood motionless, but out of the corner of his eye he saw Al inch closer to Sir Alec as his story unfolded.

"Boo hoo, Sir Alec," Al said as he scrunched up his face and pointed to it. "See? This is my sad face. Shame it didn't work out for ya'. But how'd ya' pull it off, if you were at the golf club with Freddie when Nicky was hit? Pay someone to do your dirty work, did ya'?"

Sir Alec paused, and Jake held his breath as a different and much larger drone came into view.

The only sound he could hear were the whirring blades of the drone until Sir Alec spoke. "Don't mind at all telling you how I did it," he said. "Here, let me show you, it's awfully easy." He pressed a button on his phone, and the loud blast of a gunshot rang out through the air.

Al yelled at Jake, "Now. Both men lunged forward, tackling Sir Alec and knocking him to the ground, but it was too late. Sir Alec was already dead, killed by the Smith & Wesson Model 500 handgun mounted on his own cellphone-operated drone.

# EPILOGUE

## TWO DAYS LATER

DeeDee floated on her back in the warm water of the Caribbean Sea and let it support her weight. Holding her arms at right angles to her body, she closed her eyes to the bright sunlight from above and lay there, floating like a dead man, thinking how lucky she was. *This really is paradise.*

A huge splash caused by someone diving into the water nearby sent a wave of salt water over her face and she sputtered back to reality.

"Al," Cassie called from the lower deck of the Princess Leia. "Please be careful. You almost wiped DeeDee out."

"Sorry, DeeDee." Al grinned at her and splashed her again as she swam towards the catamaran, where Jake was waiting on the deck holding out a giant towel for her.

"That's okay, Al," DeeDee said with a smile. "I've got two more days to get back at you." She grabbed the ladder hanging from the side of the boat and climbed aboard. When she was on the deck, she patted herself dry with the towel Jake handed her, stretched out on a lounge chair and placed her hands behind her head.

"I can't decide whether to read my book, have another cocktail," she sighed, "or just close my eyes and let the sun do its work on my tan. Speaking of which—" She moved a hand to shield her eyes from the sun. "Jake, can you move over a little please? You're blocking my rays."

Jake, who was standing on the deck talking to Bob, smiled. "Sorry." He stepped to the side. "Is that better?"

DeeDee nodded. "Mmm."

"I was just telling Bob the details about how Sir Alec shot himself," Jake said. "Carrying on the family tradition, so to speak. It was pretty unique the way he did it, and it was the same way he killed Nicky.

"He mounted a Smith & Wesson Model 500 pistol on the largest drone his company makes. Then he attached a miniature video camera on the drone which transmitted real time video pictures directly to his cell phone, which he used to control the drone. He could see exactly where the drone was at all times by simply looking at the video on the screen of his cell phone.

"Finally, he rigged a trigger mechanism to the pistol which could be activated by simply pushing a button on his cell phone. All he had to do when he killed Nicky was fly the drone up to within three or four feet of Nicky and fire the pistol. He didn't even have to aim when he was that close to poor Nicky. It was a straight ahead dead shot, and as soon as the pistol fired, he simply flew the drone back to his office area and landed it by remote control. The drone he used has a range of seven miles. The whole time he did this he was at the golf club with Freddie some five miles away from the scene of the murder. He used the same drone and the same process when he killed himself in front of Al and me."

"I'm glad he shot himself, and not you or Al," Cassie said from the plunge pool. "Although Al thinks it was a coward's way to go, even though Al got closure for Nicky's death. Between you and me, I think he would have preferred to have Sir Alec suffer the indignity of a murder trial and a long prison sentence. That would have really brought the family name down, which was the thing Sir Alec feared the most."

"Did I hear someone mention my name?" Al's head popped up over the top of the ladder. "Hang on, I'm coming up." The rest of his body appeared as he climbed up the last rungs of the ladder and stepped onto the deck, slapping his belly with both hands before he grabbed a towel.

Cassie groaned. "Move over, James Bond, Al De Duco's in town."

"Hey." Al grinned and sat on the edge of the plunge pool with his feet in the water. "You just gave me a great idea, Cassie. I think I'll have a vodka martini. Shaken, not stirred, please, Bob."

"Can I recommend an alternative?" Bob said. "Have you tried a Rum Point Mudslide? It's vodka, kahlua, and Bailey's Irish Cream. Legend has it that it was born at the Wreck Bar at the Rum Point Club. We Caymanians have claimed it as our own ever since."

"In that case, I think we'll all have one," Al said, looking around. "Whaddya say, Musketeers?"

They all nodded.

"I'd like to propose a toast," Al said, after Bob had brought their mudslides, which looked like chocolate milk. "To friends, and absent friends." Al lifted his glass and raised his eyes skyward.

"Friends and absent friends," the others said in unison, clinking their glasses together.

DeeDee took a sip of her mudslide and thought it tasted more like milky coffee than chocolate, but with a definite kick. "Any votes for what to do on the last two days of our trip?" she asked.

"Ima gonna' go back to Stingray City fer sure," Al said. "I wanna' get a close look at those critters if it's the last thing I do."

Cassie laughed. "They were scared of you, Al. That's why they swam in all directions when they saw you coming. They probably thought you were a sea monster."

"Watch yer' tongue, lady, or I'll show ya' what a monster throwin' his wife into the sea looks like." He leaned over and kissed her cheek. "Just kiddin'. What would you like to do, honey?"

"I'd be quite happy hanging out on the Princess Leia for the rest of my life," Cassie said, "but if Bob lets us have the use of it for the next couple of days that would be awesome."

"Whaddya' say, Bob?" Al called over to him. "What's the Friend Rate for this new vessel of yours that Nicky was kind enough to leave to you in his will, along with all the rest of his boats?"

Bob smiled. "Free for you, Al. It's a pleasure to have you all on board as my guests, and it always will be. It would make Nicky happy to know I can look after you when he's not around."

"Thanks, Bob. We appreciate it." Al drained his mudslide and set his glass down, wiping his mouth with the back of his hand. "That was good. Jake, your turn."

Jake screwed up his face. "Tough choice, but I'm going to vote for scuba diving the Babylon dive spot. It's got a corkscrew coral structure known as the Hanging Gardens that you can swim through. And I want to eat lobster one last time before we leave."

"Hey, remind me later, Jake, there's somethin' else I need to speak to ya' about." Al tapped the side of his nose twice with his forefinger. "I thought it might be a no-go with Nicky off the team, but Bob might be able to help us out."

"Sure thing," Jake said. "DeeDee, how about you?"

"Shopping," DeeDee said. "I'd like to hit the Craft Market and spend some more time in Kirk Freeport. No tax shops are always a good thing, and I still haven't bought anything for Roz."

"No problem, I'll arrange a driver for ya'," Al said. A phone on the table began to buzz, and he looked at the screen with a puzzled expression. "That's weird. I don't recognize the number," he said, picking it up.

"It's probably Devan Parker," Cassie said. "I gave her sister your number the other day rather than mine. I thought if Devan was still a person of interest, you'd want to speak to her. And if she wasn't, there was no point in her bugging me about Cayman bank accounts. My money's all in the good old US of A, where I pay tax on it, unlike some people I know."

"Gee, thanks Cassie." Al stood up. "Excuse me, folks, won't be long. Gotta take this call."

When Al returned several minutes later, Cassie looked him with concern. "Al, are you okay? You look as white as a sheet."

"I just had a bit of bad news, that's all." Al sat down and paused before continuing. "That was Benny. Three people we know, old Mob cohorts, have been whacked in the last coupla' days. Someone's out for blood."

Cassie placed a hand on Al's arm. "I'm so sorry, Al. That's a terrible blow for you, especially after what happened to Nicky."

"Yeah." Al's voice sounded old, weary. "Thing is, that's not all. Benny was callin' me with a tipoff. Word is, I'm next."

# RECIPES

## CASSAVA CAKE

**Ingredients:**
2 cups grated peeled yucca (Some supermarkets carry yucca or you can order it online.)
2 jumbo size eggs, lightly beaten
12 oz. can evaporated milk
14 oz. can sweetened condensed milk
14 oz. can coconut milk

**Directions:**
Preheat oven to 350 degrees. Combine all the ingredients and stir together in a bowl until thoroughly combined. Pour into an 8" baking dish.

Bake for one hour. Turn the oven broiler on and broil until the top of the cake is browned, 2 to 3 minutes. Remove from oven and when cool, refrigerate until ready to serve. Enjoy!

## BULLA BREAD

**Ingredients:**
2 ¾ cup sugar

½ tbsp. sea salt
2 cups water
1 cup butter, room temperature
2 tbsp. ginger
2 tbsp. vanilla extract (Don't use imitation.)
7 ½ cups flour + extra for rolling out bulla
3 tbsp. baking powder
½ tsp. baking soda
1 tsp. nutmeg

### Directions:
Preheat oven to 375 degrees. Dissolve sugar and salt in water over low heat. Add ginger, butter, and vanilla. Sift together all dry ingredients and gradually add the liquid ingredients.

Dough should be clammy and heavy. Place the dough on a flat surface and dust with flour. Roll out dough to about 1/8" thick and cut into 4" circles. Transfer rounds to cookie sheets covered with parchment paper. Bake for about 20-25 minutes. Enjoy!

**NOTE:** Traditionally these were served as a sandwich with sliced avocado as the filling.

## CONCH FRITTERS

### Ingredients:
1 quart oil for frying
1 cup all-purpose flour
1 jumbo sized egg
½ cup milk
Salt and freshly ground pepper to taste
Cayenne pepper to taste
1 cup chopped conch meat (You can purchase it online, already chopped and in a can, or you can substitute lobster or crab.)
½ medium sized white onion, chopped
½ yellow or orange pepper, chopped
2 stalks celery, chopped, leaves removed

2 cloves garlic, chopped
Ketchup, mayonnaise, and/or a dipping sauce for serving.

### Directions:

Preheat oven to 400 degrees. In a large deep pot, heat oil to 350 degrees. Mix the flour, egg, and milk in a large bowl. Season with salt, pepper, and cayenne pepper. Mix in the conch meat, onion, pepper, celery and garlic until well blended.

Drop rounded tablespoons of the mixture into the hot oil and fry until golden brown. Drain on paper towels and transfer to baking sheet. Bake in oven for 20 minutes. (Kind of weird, but if you don't put them in the oven, the insides are a little soggy.) Serve with dipping sauces.

## CONFETTI SLAW

### Ingredients:

¼ cup white wine vinegar
¼ cup olive oil
¼ cup sugar
¼ cup lime juice
½ tsp. cumin
¼ tsp. ground coriander
1/8 tsp. crushed red pepper flakes
1/8 tsp. freshly ground black pepper
6 cups thinly sliced cabbage
1 cup matchstick carrots (You can get these already prepared in the produce section of the supermarket.)
½ red bell pepper, seeds removed and thinly sliced
½ yellow bell pepper, seeds removed and thinly sliced
1 medium jalapeno chili, seeds removed and cut into thin strips
½ cup chopped fresh cilantro

### Directions:

Whisk together the vinegar, oil, sugar, lime juice, salt, cumin, coriander, red pepper flakes, and black pepper in a large bowl. Add the cabbage, carrots, red and yellow peppers and jalapeno. Toss to coat. Chill one hour in the refrigerator. Just before serving toss and stir in cilantro. Enjoy!

## MAPLE BRINED PORK CHOPS

### Ingredients:
6 cups cold water
1/3 cup Kosher salt
¾ cup maple syrup (Don't use imitation.)
2 bay leaves, crumbled
2 tbsp. black peppercorns
Six 8 oz. bone-in pork loin chops, about ¾" thick
Olive oil
Freshly ground pepper
2 tbsp. chopped chives

### Directions:
In a tall container that will fit in your refrigerator, combine the cold water, salt, maple syrup, bay leaves, and peppercorns. Submerge the pork chops in the brine and refrigerate for at least 6 hours or overnight.

Remove the pork chops from the brine, rinse them, and pat dry. Let dry on a wire rack for about 10 minutes. Discard the brine.

Heat a large cast-iron skillet over medium-high heat until very hot, about 3 minutes. Brush both sides of each chop lightly with oil and season generously with pepper. Add the chops to the pan. Cook for 2 minutes. Turn and cook for 2 minutes more.

Reduce the heat to very low and continue cooking the pork chops until done to your preference, for medium-rare about 3 minutes more each side. If using a meat thermometer, cook until the center of the chop registers 140 – 145 degrees.

Garnish with chives. Serve and enjoy!

## Paperbacks & Ebooks for FREE

Go to www.dianneharman.com/freepaperback.html and get your FREE copies of Dianne's books and favorite recipes immediately by signing up for her newsletter.

Once you've signed up for her newsletter you're eligible to win three paperbacks. One lucky winner is picked every week. Hurry before the offer ends!

## Newsletter

If you would like to be notified of her latest releases please go to www.dianneharman.com and sign up for her newsletter.

**Website:** www.dianneharman.com,
**Blog:** www.dianneharman.com/blog
**Email:** dianne@dianneharman.com

# ABOUT THE AUTHOR

Dianne lives in Huntington Beach, California, with her husband, Tom, a former California State Senator, and her boxer dog, Kelly. Her passions are cooking, reading, and dogs, so whenever she has a little free time, you can either find her in the kitchen, playing with Kelly in the back yard, or curled up with the latest book she's reading.

Her award-winning books include:

**Cedar Bay Cozy Mystery Series**

**Cedar Bay Cozy Mystery Series - Boxed Set**

**Liz Lucas Cozy Mystery Series**

**Liz Lucas Cozy Mystery Series - Boxed Set**

**High Desert Cozy Mystery Series**

**High Desert Cozy Mystery Series - Boxed Set**

**Northwest Cozy Mystery Series**

**Northwest Cozy Mystery Series - Boxed Set**

**Midwest Cozy Mystery Series**

**Midwest Cozy Mystery Series - Boxed Set**

**Jack Trout Cozy Mystery Series**

**Coyote Series**

**Midlife Journey Series**

**Red Zero Series**

**Black Dot Series**

**Cottonwood Springs Cozy Mystery Series**

**PUBLISHING 12/27/18**

**MURDER AT THE BOOKSTORE**

**BOOK FOUR OF**

**THE COTTONWOOD COVE COZY MYSTERY SERIES**

**http://getBook.at/BStore**

A woman's dream, a warning, a murder, and then the wrong person dies.

When a mistaken identity murder happens at her sister's bookstore in Cottonwood Springs, Brigid has no choice. She has to find the person who intended to murder her sister.

Her search leads her to the top of a nearby mountain to find a crazy man. Sometimes it's a good thing to have a 125-pound Newfoundland dog for a pet, particularly when the creek runs deep and fast.

This is the third book in the Cottonwood Springs series by two-time USA Today Bestselling Author, Dianne Harman, and one guaranteed to bring a smile to your face and leave a warm feeling in your heart.

Open your smartphone, point and shoot at the QR code below. You will be taken to Amazon where you can pre-order 'Murder in the Cayman Islands'.

(Download the QR code app onto your smartphone from the iTunes or Google Play store in order to read the QR code below.)

Made in the USA
San Bernardino, CA
05 March 2019